Torpor

Kieva McLaughlin

FOR DAD.

CONTENTS

1.   "THERE'S SOMETHING YOU SHOULD KNOW."

With a heavy head, James struggled to keep his eyes open long enough to figure out where he was. The last thing he recalled, he was driving towards a trendy brunch spot with Liza, his childhood best friend, who had recently become much more than that after she confessed that her feelings for him were growing stronger. He'd borrowed his mum's rusted-out Volkswagen to take her out to celebrate their sixth month of dating. While he'd never heard of a half year anniversary before, Liza insisted it was an important first milestone in any successful couple's relationship that only came around once.

James wasn't the romantic type, but he was trying to make an effort of late to keep Liza happy. They had been next door neighbours since her family had moved to England from Chicago when she was five. It was strange going from friends to much more than that, but there was nobody else he trusted like her, and she really was beautiful, maybe even the most beautiful girl in school. Certainly, the most popular. James, on the other hand, mostly kept to himself. He had got attention from some of the other girls at school before he officially started dating Liza, and he even went on the odd date with some of them. However, none of them had really aroused his full interest. Not until now. Liza was different, she was safe. She was home.

Pulling out of his memories, James slowly began to realise he was face down on the edge of the street. He could feel the hard gravel digging into his knees and hip, and a small stone was scraping the edge of his face. Forcing himself to concentrate on his surroundings, he heard the mutterings of people walking past, nobody bothering to stop and wonder how and why a 17-year-old boy had gotten there. Too disoriented to get his words out, he started calling out for help in his head, hoping that if he repeated it enough, somebody would stop.

After what could have been anywhere between five and twenty minutes, James opened his eyes and pulled himself up, his hand glued to his head trying to calm the dull jumping pain that was banging to get out. He took a good look around and realised that he was on King's Road, a busy South West London street, a fifteen-minute walk from the restaurant he was heading to. Something was off, it looked different, yet also the same, somehow. The buildings were all there more or less, but most of the shop signs had been removed or changed, and the windows, usually filled with furniture and clothing samples, were empty. Everything looked as its plainest, most basic self. Plenty of people passed by, but they didn't possess the same urgency and energy that James associated with the streets of London. Their unreadable faces, no longer stuck in their phones, gazed aimlessly into the distance.

Before he could think too much about it, a memory came flashing back, and James keeled over trying not to vomit. He had just been in an accident, or he thought he had, but if so, where was his mum's car, and more importantly, where was Liza? He remembered taking his eyes off the road for a few seconds to check a text before the car went flying down the street. *Surely, I didn't pass out?* He thought to himself. Gathering his energy, James got to his feet, anxiously looking for any signs of a crash. His mum was going to murder him if he'd damaged her car. She was already reluctant to let him drive it, but as he didn't have enough money to buy his own, he didn't give her much of a choice.

Disoriented and confused, he spun around, running his hands through his mop of dark hair, frantically trying to remember the exact place he had been driving before he had blanked and woken up on the side of the road. Subconsciously, he reached into his pocket looking for his mobile phone even though he knew it wasn't there. He'd had it in his hand before he crashed, but it wasn't anywhere in sight.

Apart from the odd glance, the people around James kept to themselves. They didn't seem perturbed or concerned with his odd behaviour and he began to wonder if he looked homeless. Once he gathered his bearings, he started to ask passers-by for help, but nobody so much as looked his way. He clutched a middle-aged man in a suit by the shoulder, who anxiously shrugged him off and walked just that much faster to get away. He turned to find a woman with a gentle face staring intently at him, a look of pity filling her eyes. She reminded him of his mum, he didn't know why, this woman was probably ten years younger, and they didn't look, act or dress alike. His mum was tall and thin and always wore colourful and eclectic clothes. This woman was short and on the chubbier side, but, all the same, she seemed like the type of person who would help him out. "Have you seen a 16-year-old girl anywhere? About a foot shorter than me with black hair and big brown eyes," he asked, his voice filled with desperation.

The woman was silent in thought for a while before replying, "There's something you should know."

She gestured across the road to an old, withered bench. Stopping himself from grunting at her for wasting time, James followed. She was the only one who seemed willing to help, and he was beginning to notice even more irregularities with his surroundings, the longer he was conscious. It was no longer cold, yet he knew it had been freezing when they'd left his house. His winter coat attested to that. Thinking about it, the grey clouds overhead had cleared up. How long had he been out? The usual London smells were also different, there was a strong scent of mustiness and the usual mix of fresh air, nature, car exhaust fumes, sewage and food had disappeared. And why were there no moving cars on the road? Since when was London completely traffic free?

Looking into his eyes, the gentle woman began to speak. Nothing could have prepared James for what she told him next, "While this may look like London in most aspects, I am afraid it's not, well not really anyway. Something significant happened to you before you passed out. What was it?" James narrowed his eyes, curious to know how she knew about the crash.

"We were driving, me and my girlfriend Liza, I only looked away from the road for a second, I swear, and before I even looked up the car was hit. Well so I thought, but there's no trace of an accident anywhere. My mum's car seems to have vanished and I've no idea where she's gone. She doesn't even know how to drive, not that she'd leave me here and take the car. How long could I have been unconscious without somebody calling an ambulance?"

"I don't like to have to be the one to tell you this but you died in that car crash. You're now in Torpor, one of the Three Worlds. Well, four if you count Earth," she hesitantly explained. When James didn't say anything, the woman continued, "When people die on Earth, they pass on to one of three places, Torpor, Tartarus or Arcadius, depending on the kind of life they lived. If your girlfriend isn't with you, she either didn't die in the same area as you did, or she wasn't destined for Torpor. You see, we appear in this world in the same spot we died at on Earth."

James didn't know whether to laugh or cry. He was wrong, this woman was nothing like his mother. He was in trouble, big trouble, and the only person who would speak to him was completely and utterly bonkers. He got up and started running, he couldn't listen to any more of this, every second he spent talking to this woman was a second he needed to spend finding Liza. He needed to get out of there. He needed to get home.

As James ran, he tried to block out the inconsistencies surrounding him, but the further he got, the harder he was finding it. The people seemed to be wandering without purpose. Nobody with a known direction or set plan of their destination in mind. He had only come across two or three moving cars, which was unheard of in London, and no planes, helicopters or even birds flew over-head. While the people sporadically interacted with each other, they didn't show much emotion, nobody seemed excited or even disgruntled, as so often he found the people in the place he called home. The colour and buzz had somehow drained out of the magical city. Even still, with no better plan, James continued home.

Forty minutes later, James was pacing up his street, out of breath and by now convinced this was all a dream. "I am unconscious. I must still be out cold from the crash," he muttered to himself, nervously pulling at his hand. If there was anywhere he was sure would be familiar, it was Clonmare Road. This was the street he'd walked up every day on the way to school, the road he'd learnt to ride his bike on and it was where he would race the cars to the corner on his roller blades on their way to work. But as James got closer to home, his family's street seemed even more out of place than anywhere else. An infrequent visitor would recognise the same brown bricked terraced houses and white painted windowsills and perhaps see no difference at all, but to James' familiar eye, the inconsistencies were glaring. Maybe it was because he knew it best of all and was sure that Mrs Power would never have got rid of the mountain of flowers that filled her front windows, or that the Green family wouldn't have traded their Toyota jeep for a rundown van and a motorbike, and he was certain that Mr Russo would be six foot under before he gave up the parking space, that was just the right distance from his house, to charge up his electric taxi. James made the mistake of parking there after a late night at Liza's, only to be woken up two hours later by a very worked up Italian man that had just come off his night shift.

With bated breath, James approached his front gate. From the outside, his small but homely house didn't look like it had been lived in for some time. While it didn't look neglected, there were no cars or even bins outside, and most of the windows were free from curtains or blinds. He walked up to the front window and peered inside. Surprisingly, there was a small amount of furniture in the living room, but none of it was familiar. None of it was the furniture he had grown up with. He turned the front door handle, and to his amazement, the door opened. Leaving doors unlocked in London was a risk his Mum and Dad would definitely never take.

While this was his home, James felt like a stranger, so he called out to announce himself before he went inside to avoid any awkward or hostile run-ins, "Is anybody there? Mum, Dad, Jen? It's James." As expected, nobody responded. James carefully stepped inside, creaking on the hallway's old wood. "Where is our carpet gone, and when did we paint the walls grey?" he mumbled to himself quietly. "Mum would never allow it, she loves colour and character too much." He quickly noticed that the many family photos that usually littered the hall's walls, making the house a home, had been removed. He continued into the living room and took a better look at the furniture he had spied through the window; a single burgundy sofa, a fireplace and an old rotting wooden table. All the nuances of his family home were gone; his father's coffee stained leather armchair that he refused outright to swap for a new one because it now moulded perfectly to his shape, the small grey tv that he and his older sister Jen fought for control over every night, before she moved to Brighton for University. Even his carved name on the fireplace was nowhere to be seen. He had been grounded for a month for doing that a few years before.

As James wandered around his former house, he started to lose the anxious feeling that had slowly grown in the pit of his stomach since he'd woken up. His uncertainty and nervousness about what was happening were turning into frustration, and his frustration was turning into anger. *Where were his things? And where were his family?* He needed answers, and he wasn't going to get them here. This was clearly no longer the home he had grown up in, and he felt the sudden urge to remove himself from it. Storming out of Jen's bedroom, that was missing any and everything that reminded him of her, he made his way out of the unfamiliar house and hopped the wall over to Liza's next door. He had a strong feeling that she wouldn't be there, but he needed to check for himself anyway.

Just like his house, Liza's door was left unlocked. James walked inside, this time, not bothering to introduce himself. Unlike his house, her furniture was gone, and nothing was left in its place. He ran upstairs to check her bedroom, but it too was empty. He decided to go banging on the neighbour's doors until he found an answer that he was willing to accept. An answer that didn't involve crazy delusions of death and an afterlife. By now, he was sure he wouldn't find any familiar faces or belongings residing in their houses, but it was a better alternative than sitting and waiting for something to happen. However, just as he began to storm out the door, he spotted someone that dragged at his attention. It was the same woman who had spoken to him on the street, and she was lingering outside near the neighbour's garden gate. She looked relieved to see him.

"You again. How do you know where I live? Why are you following me?" James asked, marching towards her, his voice filled with accusation.

"James, I know this is hard to digest, it's a lot, but now that you've seen more and come to this house, maybe you can start to come around to what I've told you," she pleaded.

"James? How do you..." he trailed off. He knew how she knew his name before he even asked. It was the same reason as why she reminded him of his mum when he had first approached her. A memory of her appeared to him from when he was younger, which snowballed into memories that spanned years of his childhood. She was a friend of his mums, they used to spend endless days and nights filling his house with chatter and laughter. They were unlikely friends who didn't have much in common. She was the more reserved and traditional type, and his mum was eccentric and out there. His dad never understood the match, but he was thankful his wife had a calming influence in her life. She had died from cancer when James was eight or so. His mum was heartbroken after that, she wasn't the same for weeks. She still occasionally talked of her, always very fondly, when something brought her back to the years of friendship they'd spent together.

"I died," James announced astonished, more to himself than anyone else. He walked inside, into the living room and took a seat on the foreign sofa. "How can this be? I'm only seventeen. You're not supposed to die as a teenager."

The woman smiled gently and sat next to him, "When people first get here, they more often than not have the same reaction. Particularly those who are young, or people who died in freak accidents on Earth. People that didn't get the time to come to terms with their passing. I am Tracey, Tracey Flores, you were probably too young to remember me all that well, but I remember you like I was only in your kitchen yesterday. You are James Moore; your parents are Caroline and Dave. Your mum and I grew up together, I can't imagine what she's going through without you."

James didn't want to think about the people he'd left behind just yet, he needed to focus on understanding his surroundings, "Tell me more about this place, what did you call it?" he questioned.

"This is Torpor, one of the Three Worlds. It probably feels a bit like an afterlife to you, but in reality, this is life now, but with no death. There's no ending. Earth is sort of like a testing ground for figuring out where you belong."

If Liza wasn't with James, she must be in one of the other worlds, unless she survived the crash, he thought hopefully before blocking it from his mind. This wasn't the time for positive thinking, Liza could be in real danger.

"How can I get to these other worlds? I need to find Liza, she'll be lost without me. It's all my fault that we crashed, if I just hadn't looked at my phone," he vented regretfully.

"I'm sorry James, but Arcadius and Tartarus are out of bounds. Residents can't travel from world to world, only The Controller and his Whiteflyers can."

"Who?" James asked, before realising he didn't care who The Controller or his Whiteflyers were. "Actually, never mind who, just tell where I can find this Controller." James demanded, frustrated at how long it was taking to get answers.

"He's the leader of the Three Worlds and he lives in Arcadius. Unsurprisingly, the best out of the three worlds is where he calls home. But even if he was here, you wouldn't be able to get an audience with him. It's just not how things work around here. We are irrelevant to him."

James didn't know what to say, there was so much to take in. Way too much. How could he never see her again? He needed to make sure she was okay, to reassure her that she wasn't completely alone, that she still had him. He was never really that religious, but this world, Torpor, didn't sound like anything he'd been told at Church when he was younger about what happened to people when they died. Heaven was supposed to be fun and rewarding from what he had gathered, and he was supposed to be with his family and friends that had died before him. If he understood Tracey correctly, this wasn't even the after, not really, Earth was just the before.

When James didn't say anything for a while, Tracey suggested another way he might find Liza, "If you remember, I told you earlier that you appear in Torpor in the same place you died on Earth. If Liza didn't die with you, if she was brought to a hospital and died there, she may still be in Torpor. I can go with you." For the first time since he had woken up, James felt a sense of hope, he had something to strive towards, something to focus on.

"Thanks for your help so far, but I think I'll go there alone. I need some time to process everything you have explained to me." He felt guilty for not accepting her help, she seemed lonely, like she needed a friend, but while she was a familiar face in a foreign place, he didn't really remember her all that well, and he was used to solving problems by himself, he liked it best that way.

The closest hospital that James could remember was Chelsea Westminster. His Dad had taken him there when he'd split his head open five years previously. He'd been unsuccessfully trying to read his homework book while cycling when he'd crashed into a parked van. His mum had been too panicked at the sight of the blood running down his neck to even come to the hospital. She was the dramatic sort when it came to her children. James touched his hand to the back of his head remembering. He was still missing a patch of hair that never grew back over the scar. He wasn't one hundred percent sure how to get to the hospital, and unfortunately, without mobiles, this world didn't have digital maps, but he had a general idea that if he got to the river, he could make his way from there.

2. "I'LL COME WITH YOU."

In stark contrast to the unexcitable outside world, the local hospital was manic. James hadn't visited there on Earth for quite some time, so was unsure of how different this one would look and feel to the newly dead. However, he was sure that the panic that was playing out in front of him wouldn't help to settle their nerves, and it would only encourage people to act erratically. A grey haired man in a hospital gown and no shoes and a middle aged woman with a knotted mass of hair rushed around in a frenzy looking for a familiar face, something to prove they weren't going mad. Another lady hid her face in her hands and rocked back and forth in a ball, in the hopes that the dark would transport her back to the reality that she knew. There was, however, a silent majority, that at first James hadn't noticed, acting just as the people on the streets had. Placid, untemperamental, and if he was honest, just plain bored.

James carefully looked around deciding where he'd be most likely to find Liza. Luckily, he spotted a hospital sign that directed him around the hospital, so the lack of receptionists wasn't that inconvenient. He decided that the Accident & Emergency department and then the ICU were the most logical first places to begin his search to find her, so he exited the front doors and made his way to the attached smaller building next door, hopeful that he'd see her familiar curly locks among the craziness.

A&E had a different energy about it than the main hospital had. There were plenty of people sitting on the lined up red plastic chairs in the waiting area, but none of them seemed to be the confused and disoriented people that he now associated with the newly dead. *Surely there's no need for functional hospitals anymore now that we have died, what are these people waiting for?* he thought to himself, not wanting to talk to the surrounding array of strangers to ask them what they were doing there. He was never the inquiring type. He preferred to figure things out himself. He had always been somewhat of an introvert who liked to keep his thoughts private. His mum had always said he'd got it from his father, who was quiet and focused. He was the kind of man who did not get mad much, but if he did, you knew you were in trouble. His parents were a strange pairing in some ways, but both filled in the gaps that the other was missing in life.

Through the main doors, James optimistically looked into each of the carefully marked emergency rooms, but to his disappointment, all of them were empty, without so much as a window to look out of. He made his way up to the ICU, hoping he'd have better luck there. He was sure that was where all of the serious hospital cases ended up, so if Liza was close to death when they brought her in, there was a big chance that that's where he would find her. Like the A&E, the ICU was filled with people sitting and standing around waiting. Ignoring the zombielike bystanders, James made his way into each of the rooms, closing his eyes and holding his breath before he opened each door. While some of these rooms did hold the odd piece of furniture, there was no sign of Liza. Starting to lose his patience, James turned to leave the last room, but at the last second, he hesitated. There was something different about the air filling the centre of the room. Just above the lone piece of furniture sitting there, a white metal hospital bed, the air was fuzzy, heavier. It was almost like he was looking at it through wet glass. He walked over to examine it, reaching out his hand to brush through the inconsistencies. To his surprise, an invisible force wouldn't allow him to penetrate it. The air was almost frozen in place. He pushed down hard, determined to seize an element of control over something, he was fed up of feeling useless, like he wasn't in charge of what he did or of what happened with his life. Despite his efforts, the space of blurred air wouldn't budge, but only moments later he realised why. A girl appeared.

James took a few steps back not wanting to frighten her, he guessed he'd just witnessed someone arriving to Torpor after they had died on Earth. She hadn't yet opened her eyes or sat up, she didn't seem conscious. As far as he could tell, Torpor's newest resident looked to be a similar age to him. The long wavy auburn hair that rested on her stomach was highlighted further by the contrast of her sallow skin. He contemplated leaving. He didn't want to be the one to explain to her what had happened to her. He didn't even really understand this world and what was going on himself, but something in his head was beckoning him to stay.

After a few minutes, the girl opened her eyes. She stared at James with big brown eyes for what seemed like forever before she jumped back in fright. "Where am I? Who are you?" she exclaimed, looking around the room for the answers to her questions. As James gazed down at her atop the hospital bed, she asked, "Are you a doctor? You seem awfully young." James didn't know what to say so he turned to leave, it was a mistake to wait for her to wake up. "No please don't leave. Tell me what's going on," she pleaded, holding her hand to her throat, almost out of breath. James halted, his thoughts whizzing through his brain. He remembered clearly how he had felt, only earlier that day, when nobody would stop to help him, so he turned back towards her, deciding to talk her through everything. Well everything that he knew anyway.

The new girl, who had introduced herself as Stevie Miller, seemed to take the news that she had died pretty well. She didn't go through the five stages of grief that James had and, instead, jumped straight to acceptance. He noticed she'd purposely dodged around the circumstances of her own death, but from her reaction to the news, James had figured she must have had some idea that she was going to die and had come to terms with it before she passed. That was a nice surprise, considering he didn't deal very well with emotions and wasn't skilled in the art of comforting, particularly with people that he didn't know.

While Stevie's reaction to her death was surprising, yet somehow understandable, her reaction to Torpor and the other worlds was just downright strange, "This is seriously cool, it's like we've been thrown into an unrealistic high budget movie. I mean, I've been an atheist of sorts for years now. Can anyone really be sure that there's something after we die?"

James didn't think of it in the same way. While he was not religious, deep down he presumed something must happen when people die. He could never have believed that there was just nothing, and this world didn't live up to his, admittedly unvoiced, expectations.

"Erm okay… that's not the response I had, but I suppose things could be worse. From the sound of it, things certainly are worse in Tartarus, which is why I can't really stay and chat now that I can see how well you are taking everything. I woke up in this world alone, but when I died, I was with someone, and I need to check the rest of the hospital to make sure she's safe. Maybe you had a home on Earth you can go to? You could check there for people you know that have died."

At his last sentence, James thought he saw Stevie's face show a brief moment of realisation, but it vanished just as quickly as it arrived. "Wait. I'll come with you," she exclaimed, jumping off the bed enthusiastically. While James didn't want his mum's friend Tracey tagging along, there was something about Stevie that he found comfort in. She was in the same situation as he was and her ease and relaxed mood with everything was reassuring, so he didn't object.

As they roamed the mostly empty corridors and rooms in the hospital, James listened to Stevie's many elaborate stories of the life she lived before she arrived here. He wasn't sure they were completely true, but he was happy to listen and take his mind off the present. She steered clear of stories that were too personal and instead explained, in detail, her adventures travelling the world with her pilot dad, "I wouldn't join him on every holiday of course, but for a lot of the really special places or if I was on my school holidays, he would let me. My favourite has to be Hawaii. I've been there lots of times, we go scuba diving there every year."

James hadn't travelled overseas much, his family couldn't afford it, but he had been to Spain once or twice, and he often visited Ireland in the summer to see his Granny Mc, as they called her. During the school holidays his mum couldn't take much time off work, so Granny Mc would mind him and his sister Jen. Although not as extravagant as the United States, Africa or Asia, the times he spent in Donegal, in the North of the country, made up some of his favourite memories. His mum's mum would organise plays, dances and singalongs in her front room, using her mountain of fur coats and their late grandad's old suits as props, and at night they'd push the couches together to make one big bed and stay up until the early hours of the morning listening to the tales of their grandmother's past.

After what felt like hours of searching the hospital grounds, James was finding it harder and harder to distract himself with Stevie's stories of visiting the Great Pyramid of Giza and bumping into her favourite actress while shopping on Rodeo Drive. Impatiently, he looked down at his watch to check how much time was left to search for Liza before nightfall. "My watch has stopped. What does yours say?" he asked Stevie, abruptly tapping his watch with the tip of his index finger.

She answered, not even bothering to look down at her own, "Yeah mine doesn't work either, I noticed it a few floors ago. I guess there's no need to tell the time here. When we have forever, what's the rush?" At that, James felt a sunken feeling weigh down his stomach. While he was happy there was something after death, the small amount of time that he'd spent in Torpor didn't reassure him that it would satisfy him forever.

"So, what now?" Stevie asked when they'd thoroughly checked the hospital. "I don't think she's here; we've checked everywhere once and the most likely places twice. Do you want to recheck her house?"

Deflated, James realised she was right, they'd spent so much time walking around the hospital that he'd even figured out what the people waiting in the A&E and at the hospital entrance were doing. They were waiting for the living to die, to be reunited with their loved ones. The most depressing part of that wasn't how useless they must have thought their existence was that that's all they could do with their day, it was that two thirds of their loved ones wouldn't be coming to Torpor at all. A lot of those waiting could be anticipating the arrival of friends and family that were already in Arcadius and Tartarus.

"What about you?" James asked Stevie on their way out of the hospital.

She looked at him defensively, "What about me?"

"I just mean, surely there's somewhere you want to go. How about we check out where your house is? If we can even call it your house anymore, I know I wouldn't consider mine my house anymore. It's getting dark now anyway and this world is creepy enough in the daylight."

Stevie looked at him for a moment before nodding, "I can't imagine we will find anyone I know there but I suppose it can't hurt."

Stevie's house was nothing like James had experienced first-hand before. It sat on one of the up-market, fancy streets of South Kensington. It was where the people from around his Granny's area pictured when he told them he lived in London. He never corrected them, but he always felt slightly ashamed of hiding the truth when he got home. His mum and dad worked hard for their house and they never went hungry or without new clothes. Stevie's three-story house was painted white, with a big black door that matched the surrounding gates. The top floor held little balconies outside the tall windows that left James picturing privileged people sitting on them sipping tea while reading their morning paper. The front gardens weren't decorated very well, but James had passed similar houses on Earth, and he'd put money on it that they were usually decorated with vast amounts of flowers and that some would even hold statues and fountains.

"Well, I see you weren't making up the stories about travelling around the world," James teased, elbowing her lightly in jest. Stevie raised her eyebrow and shook her head, which inadvertently made her head of auburn hair dance around her shoulders, prompting butterflies to dance in James' stomach. Awkwardly, he clutched his side and led the way into the house.

Unlike James' house, this place immediately seemed like it was being lived in. There was a lot more furniture than his house had, and there were small luxuries like blankets and pillows tossed around the place. There was even a white pair of men's shoes laid out in the hallway. Stevie looked at him knowingly, and they silently agreed to be quiet and stick together until they figured out whether or not the house was empty. While James moved from room to room with caution, looking for signs of life, he couldn't help but appreciate the inside of the Miller family home. It was just as spectacular as the outside. High ceilings and decorated walls adorned every room, and the marbled bathroom floors and walk-in wardrobes were things that James had only ever seen on television. He silently wondered about Stevie and the life she had lived before dying, and most prominently, he wondered how she died.

Walking into the kitchen with Stevie dragging behind, and seeing the empty kitchen cupboards, James realised something for the first time since he woke up in Torpor. He didn't feel hungry.-Stevie confirmed the same, "No, not even slightly. Actually, I'm surprised I haven't noticed before, I really do love food." Stevie's slender body didn't attest to her love for food, but James was learning to expect the unexpected when it came to his new acquaintance. Watching her effortlessly perch herself on top of the kitchen counter, he realised how quickly he was taking to her. He wasn't the most open person when it came to making new friends and bar Liza, and a couple of other close friends at home, there weren't many people that he really got on with. It wasn't like he actively fought with people, but he felt a sense of ease at being alone. Something was different about Stevie though, she brought out a calm in him that wasn't released very easily.

Before he dwelt on it too much, Stevie interrupted his thought process, "We may not need to eat in this world, but I am starting to get tired, so I guess we still need to sleep. Should we find some sort of beds for the night before we restart the hunt for your girlfriend tomorrow? I know another hospital we could potentially try and I know you said you've checked her house, but I don't see the harm in checking it again. If she died after you she could have arrived there when you had left and it's not like we've time to lose," Stevie asked, a yawn materialising on her mouth just as she finished.

"You go to sleep. I'll stay up and take the first watch. I don't feel comfortable here yet, this house seems lived in, even if there's nobody here," James suggested, subtly urging Stevie to get some rest by nodding his head towards the living room.

An hour later, James had joined Stevie in the front room. He told himself he wanted something to sit on that wasn't made of wood, but truth be told there was something eerie about this world that didn't sit right with him. He didn't like the thought of separating. For the first time since he had met Stevie, he had nothing to distract himself with and he couldn't get his mind off Liza. Images of what Tartarus might look like floated in and out of his mind, giving him pangs of anxiety and anger. Fire and darkness consumed him. Even more terrifyingly, he imagined the people, murderers and thieves. *She couldn't be there, she wouldn't be there,* he told himself over and over. He closed his eyes and slowly counted to ten, trying to calm his nerves, but when he opened them, Stevie was gone. Jumping up, James ran to the kitchen and out into the hall. The front door was ajar, and he thought he could see someone through the stained-glass window standing out the front. "Stevie, have you gone mad? I thought we decided to stay inside," he called out as he paced down the hall after her. He was halfway there when a gust of wind blew the front door open. It wasn't Stevie.

"Liza? Is that you?" James mumbled, slowing himself down as he cautiously stepped outside. The girl didn't turn and instead continued to slowly cross the road outside of Stevie's house. He stared at her tightly curled black hair, it was showing rare glimpses of brown that bright lights often revealed. In realisation, James whipped his head to the right to confirm where the light was coming from. A rusted silver car, just like the one his mum drove, was pelting down the road. Turning towards him, Liza let out a piercing scream for help, terror painted on her otherwise immaculate face. "Not again. Please, not again," he cried as he ran towards her. *BANG.*

James' eyes snapped open. He was covered in sweat and his heart was pounding. He looked to his left and took a deep, reassuring breath at the site of a sleeping Stevie… He was only dreaming, he had dozed off. Shivers ran through his body and he shook himself off, stretching his arms out, trying to rid himself of such a nightmare. "Put your hands down and don't move," came a stern, quiet voice from behind him. Doing as he was told, James lowered his hands, simultaneously eyeing the gold-plated mirror above the fireplace. He could see the reflection of a very sturdy looking man in his early 50's staring at the couch where he and Stevie lay. The man had a shaved head and was dressed head to toe in pristine white, he looked almost clinical. But what bothered James most about this man wasn't how he looked or dressed, it was the small ball of fire that was seemingly coming out of his index finger. "Turn around."

3. "THERE IS NO GOING BACK."

"So, who wants to explain to me why you're both in my sleeping quarters? Are you looking to have a target put on your heads or are you just insane?" the unusual man angrily demanded from James and a now awoken and very alert Stevie.

Before James could think of what to say or do, Stevie jumped up to face him and began, "I don't know who you are but this was my house only this morning, before I died and arrived in this strange yet wonderful world. So, whose house it is can really be seen as a matter of perspective. Wouldn't you agree?" James assumed the man wasn't used to being answered to so frankly by the look of perplexion and growing frustration on his face.

"No, it's not a matter of perspective, it's a matter of I say... and you get moving out of here," he declared, simultaneously moving his thumb in the direction of the door. "Hmm, thanks but I think we will have to gracefully decline and ask that you get mov..." Stevie began before she was cut short by the unbelievable sight in front of her.

The man was rising into the air as the small ball of fire on his middle finger expanded.

He cleared his throat and grunted angrily, "I know you haven't been here very long, but in Torpor, I rule the residents, me and the other Whiteflyers. As you will see, I am one of the more understanding ones. A few of my less tolerant colleagues would have already set you on fire and thrown you through the wall by now for talking to them like that. I, on the other hand, am going to give you a ten second head start."

At the word 'Whiteflyers', James' stomach sank. Tracey had briefly mentioned them alongside The Controller but had conveniently forgotten to mention the whole fire and flying thing. If they worked for the leader of this world, they weren't the people to get on the wrong side of. Not if he wanted to find Liza anyway. He cursed himself for not finding out more about them when he had had the chance.

Before Stevie could say anything else to get them in even more trouble, James jumped in, "Apologies for getting in your way. As my friend Stevie here was just saying, we've only been here for a day, and we haven't been told the rules around here yet. We were just checking out her old house to get a better idea of what's going on. We'll leave now." The man seemed to relax at that and lowered himself down. But even still, he didn't extinguish the growing fire that was by now covering his hand and slowly travelling up his arm. It almost looked like he himself was up in flames, but James noticed a thin layer of air between his arm and the fire that seemed to be protecting his clothes.

As James turned to leave, pushing a reluctant Stevie ahead of him, the man called after them, "If you're at Trafalgar Square tomorrow, a bit after sunrise, you'll get a better understanding of how things work around here." With a brief nod of recognition, James continued out the door.

With nowhere else to go, the two of them headed back to Clonmare Road. There was furniture in his house when he'd been there before, which made James suspect that it would be housing more unexpected guests that they might have to answer to now that it was nightfall. However, Liza's house was empty last he checked, so he hoped it would be the safer option until they could get more answers when the sun came up. "I still don't know why we had to leave mine. We should be making a dominant first impression here, or they'll think we are weak. Have you never heard of the prison mentality? You're supposed to challenge the biggest guy you can see before anyone decides you're weak," Stevie complained as they got settled on the floor of the empty living room. James couldn't bring himself to make use of the bedrooms. It felt strange enough just sleeping in the same room as Stevie in Liza's house. He felt like he shouldn't be enjoying spending time with Stevie as much as he was with Liza still missing, but he couldn't face this world alone, and she was starting to feel like a good friend. Even though they'd just met, this adversity they were going through together was speeding up their friendship.

Sarcastically, James replied with a hint of laughter, "Yeah, because your intimidating words are definitely a match for his otherworldly, or should I say, 'this worldly', superpowers."

Stevie's eyes lit up at the word superpowers, and James wasn't surprised at her fascination with the display that had just been put on for them. "So, you don't think it was an illusion? Neither do I. Nobody is that good a magician," Stevie said excitedly.

"Yeah it seemed pretty real alright. Can this day get any weirder?" James speculated aloud.

"I wonder what else they can do. And where do I find these powers? Maybe we have them too but just don't know how to use them. Did that woman you were talking to earlier mention them?" Stevie asked before gulping the air she was too preoccupied to inhale as she spoke.

"No, she didn't mention them, but I didn't really give her the chance. I guess we will find out tomorrow."

As he dozed off to sleep for the last couple of hours before the day arrived, James' mind went to other places, speculating on the other possible powers the Whiteflyers, and possibly everyone in Torpor, could have.

As James stretched out and gradually began to open his eyes, he thought for a split second that he was back at home in bed. He imagined his mum downstairs dancing while she made the family breakfast and his dad watching the TV, trying to catch the morning headlines before he rushed off to work. He could almost smell the smoky bacon and hear the snotty morning presenter complaining about something or other.

However, his daydream only lasted a few seconds before he was brought back to reality with a bright and cheery welcome from Stevie, "Wakey, wakey sleepy head. We have a long day ahead of us of finding your girlfriend and figuring out where we can sign up for those superpowers. I can picture us now, Batman and Robin. I'd be Batman obviously, you're too quiet and mysterious to be the leading part." James guessed that he wasn't the only one who went to bed with superpowers on his brain from her raised eyebrow and the cheeky grin on her face.

Although he didn't feel unclean, he wasn't even sure sweating was a thing in Torpor, James felt a hot shower would start the day off right. Yesterday was a bit of a mess and he wanted today to go a lot more smoothly, he needed it to if he was going to find out more about where Liza was. There were no shower gels or shampoos in Liza's parent's bathroom, but water ran out of the shower head, so James undressed and stared at himself in the small round mirror above the sink, waiting for the water to heat up. Looking at himself, he thought of his sister Jen. They had the same hazel eyes, dark brown hair and palish skin. He smiled to himself looking up at his eyebrows, she always made fun of his grown out bushy hairs and often begged him to let her tidy them up. Now he'd give anything to be back with her, even if it meant letting her tweeze them.

As James got into the shower, he allowed himself, for the first time since he died, to properly register what his family must be feeling about his passing. He was reckless to check his phone while he was driving, but he never imagined for a second that he wasn't in total control of the car. He prided himself on being a great driver. His mum would be in bed inconsolable, she didn't take bad news well, especially when it came to her children. His dad would be no use in helping her cope with it all either. He would go quiet for some time, try to deal with it inside. He'd resort to long walks away from the house, spending hours away from the family at a time. Jen would have to take James' usual role of protecting the house until everyone came to terms with his death. He was sure she would move home for a while until their lives got back on track. If Liza was still alive, she would probably still be in hospital considering the crash was bad enough to kill him, he wasn't sure if she would even be awake yet.

The thought angered James, he was helpless. He hopped out of the shower and re-joined Stevie downstairs. It was time for answers.

Stevie and James arrived at Trafalgar Square just as the sun came up. Thousands of people were piled around the two fountains, the dark metal lions and the tall column that James couldn't remember the name of. They were waiting for something, but what that something was Stevie and James were still unsure of. Getting there was the farthest they had to travel since arriving to Torpor and the London Underground was apparently not something that had made it from Earth to their new home. James made a mental note to ask The Controller about that when he finally got an audience. Their travel was shortened considerably though after finding two children's bikes in one of the many parks they cut across. James briefly thought about using one of the cars parked on the sides of the roads, but he had seen very few moving since he woke up here, so thought it was best to leave the unknowns until after the meeting, or announcement, or whatever it was the Whiteflyer they had come across was sending them to. They'd learnt their lesson about doing as they pleased after arriving at Stevie's house unannounced and most definitely uninvited.

Even though he'd witnessed the London streets the day before, the sight of the unexcitable residents roaming the streets of Torpor still unsettled James. Although, with fresh eyes, he did notice that this time there were a few people that stood out from the rest, people that hadn't given up just yet. They still smiled and moved with some sort of determination. He had even seen some of them laugh. In most cases these people weren't alone, he guessed their family and closest friends had ended up in Torpor with them, or maybe they just hadn't been there as long as the others had and the novelty of doing nothing still hadn't worn off. He knew most people on Earth, given the option, would do anything for a few weeks away from their usual responsibilities, with no school or work or worries. Summer couldn't come quicker for James every year when he could get away from early mornings and homework. A lot of the people gathering at Trafalgar Square seemed to have a similar sort of attitude. They stood around quietly chatting amongst themselves, waiting for something to happen. It was nothing compared to what James would usually expect from gatherings of that size though. It reminded him more of strangers queuing for the tube at rush hour than it did the crowds that waited to get admitted to a football stadium or a concert. However, from what James had seen from Torpor so far, it was buzzy.

"Any idea what's going on here?" Stevie asked an impatient older man next to them, who was looking around and scowling at some of the louder bystanders. He didn't come across as clueless in comparison to some of the other people surrounding them, nor was he even slightly excited.

He looked at her for a few seconds, deciding whether or not he would bother answering before shaking his head, rolling his eyes to the sky, "The Whiteflyers gather here once a week to read out a list containing the names of the people that have died in London and come to Torpor this week. Most of the people here are waiting to hear if their family and friends have come. Others are new and want to know more about how this world works, how it's run. I am guessing the two of you fall into the latter category. When you've been here for a while it gets easy to spot the new arrivals." James' heart jumped, this is what he'd been waiting to hear since he had arrived at Torpor, a way to find out if Liza had too.

Before James could ask for more information, a loud bell rang through the square, quieting the people in the crowd and giving them a nudge to face forward. James turned around to see forty odd men and women coming out of the doors of what James had always known as the National Art Gallery. It was an old English building held up by roman style pillars, with a domed entrance spouting two stairs. He had even visited it once on a school trip when he was younger. The men and women were all dressed completely in white, and all but three of them looked for ways to intimidate the onlookers by showcasing their powers. Some of the Whiteflyers glided just above the ground, negating the need for walking. Others decided they'd show off by playing with fire instead. One even summoned a ball of water from the fountain to James' left and caught it in his mouth. The three that didn't show off their powers stood at the front. James immediately decided they were in charge. In his experience, the most successful and secure people didn't see the need to prove it to anyone.

"There he is, beside the young man in the middle," Stevie whispered to James.

James didn't need to ask who she was talking about, the scene with the bald man from Stevie's the night before had been replaying in his head all day, "So, I guess he wasn't lying about the other Whiteflyers setting us on fire and throwing us through the walls, they don't seem like the understanding type."

The woman to the left of the man in the middle of the entrance began to speak, and as she did the rest of the Whiteflyers quickly extinguished their flames and came back to the ground. Her voice carried across the square with no help from a microphone or a megaphone. It wasn't that it was any louder, but it sounded like she was next to them as she spoke. "Residents of Torpor, another week has passed, and another few hundred of you have joined us. To those of you that includes, welcome. To everyone else, welcome back."

James listened to the rest of her speech patiently waiting to hear Liza's name, but the new resident's names were called, and the only two names he recognised were James Moore and Stevie Miller. He'd almost forgotten that they'd be called themselves and felt a little eerie about the finality of it all. There was no denying that he had died anymore. After having no luck at the crash site, at home and at the hospital, he wasn't really expecting to hear Liza's name deep down, but it stung, nonetheless.

After the woman finished what she had to say, the man beside her began to speak. As he did, he somehow manipulated the ground beneath him to rise into the air, demanding the absolute attention of the audience, "For those new to Torpor, this is one of the Three Worlds. You are here because your time on Earth was satisfactory enough to avoid Tartarus, but nonetheless it was too forgettable to meet the standards of Arcadius. You are neither good nor bad, evil nor saintly. In most cases, I would go as far as to say your existence was meaningless, it likely had no impact on anything around you. Earth will move on just as if you were never there."

"Well that's a lovely way to put it. They should have begun with that, I feel super welcome now," Stevie interrupted loud enough to make a few people nearby giggle.

The man continued, evidently his hearing didn't travel like his voice did, or maybe he just wasn't fazed by the bystander's comments, "Each world, including Torpor, is ruled by us, the Whiteflyers, we are the law here. What we say is absolute, and it can only be challenged by The Controller himself. As you have just seen, we command the powers of Air, Water, Fire and Earth. Cross us at your own discretion. However, we are here to keep order, and the best interests of Torpor are at the heart of what we say and do, so there should be no reason, other than personal gain, for anyone to disobey us."

At that, the old man Stevie had spoken to before grunted and turned to address them, "That's William Hatt. He is well respected among the Whiteflyers because he has been here since the 1600s. Around here he's known and addressed as just 'Hatt'," he explained, putting emphasis on the word 'Whiteflyers' to make it clear that the other residents weren't as big fans. James also noticed that a few of the people around them were shaking their heads, but the majority continued to look on, which he guessed was out of fear.

Hatt continued, "Nobody in Torpor has the right to own anything including property, what was yours on Earth is forfeit, we are equals. What's mine is yours and what's yours is mine. If you want to sleep or reside in a building, there is nobody stopping you from doing so, but you cannot decide who else chooses to reside there either. The only building that is out of bounds is the one behind me. Much goes on behind these doors, that is unfit for your unworthy ears."

"Ha! That's rich," Stevie mumbled under her breath, most likely thinking about being kicked out of her house the night before.

The rest of Hatt's speech continued along the same path, laying out the rules and regulations to the residents of Torpor. Surprisingly, the cars weren't mentioned as being prohibited, so James assumed the reason they were rarely used was down to the fact that people weren't pushed for time. What was the use of cars when you weren't constricted by it? Before the display was over, the strict looking woman made a final announcement that got some of the onlookers excited, "Next week we will begin taking applications for the annual Whiteflyer initiation. Those of you who think they have what it takes to join the ranks of the elite, and do the bidding of The Controller himself, will get their chance to prove they are more than the worthless imprint they have made on Earth." At this, a bell rang to announce the end of the meeting. Everyone scattered as the

Whiteflyers retreated into the building behind them. James assumed that it was no longer the National Art Gallery and more likely some sort of Whiteflyer headquarters or a meeting building.

"So that's three things we've learnt today, your girlfriend definitely isn't here, Whiteflyers are jerks, and... we need to sign up to be one," Stevie recited to James as they pushed through the crowd and made their way out of the square.

"Join them, are you mad? They're power hungry morons, why would we join them?" James asked, astonished that Stevie would want to feed into the bureaucracy of this world. He wanted their powers just as much as she did, but he wasn't willing to pay the price of becoming a Whiteflyer and tormenting the residents of Torpor to be able to get them.

Stevie looked at him like he had ten heads, "Weren't you listening to that Hatt guy's rules? Regular residents can't get into Arcadius and Tartarus, and Liza isn't here. If you want to find her, we need access to the other worlds."

"And you're willing to go through all of that just to help me find her?" James threw back at her, finding it hard to believe that Stevie's reasons were completely selfless.

"You're not the only one looking for people here. You're not the only one that has lost someone," Stevie responded in a very finalised tone, before speeding up ahead so she wouldn't have to explain anything further.

Six days later, Stevie and James had become a lot more accustomed to life in Torpor. They'd just about got used to the miserable people that walked the streets and they had turned Liza's house into a home of sorts, or at least a base where they could sleep and relax when they weren't out exploring. James was right about not going back to his flat the night they'd met their first Whiteflyer, a friendly older lady slept there at night after spending her days in the hospitals waiting for her husband. In true Stevie fashion, she often stopped and chatted with their neighbour, Anne, if they ran into her as she left the house in the morning or on her way home. By the sounds of things, Anne's husband was most likely already in Arcadius or Tartarus, but the optimistic woman preferred to live in denial with a sliver of hope, than face the fact that she'd never see him again. Only the morning before she stared up at James and announced proudly that he was turning 105 at the end of the month. After this, the fact that he may never see Liza again rang true for the hundredth time since James had died.

Since Trafalgar Square the week before, James and Stevie spent most of their time exploring Torpor. While it was a translation of the London they'd grown up in, it still took a lot of getting used to and they really didn't have much else to do. It was surprising how much of your day was freed up when eating and drinking were removed. He couldn't help but laugh about what his mum's reaction would be when she found out her Friday night bottle of wine was prohibited. Stevie and James had spent a lot of time talking about their previous lives and excitedly fantasising together about what would come from their next experience with the Whiteflyers once they had signed up to become one.

Until now, Stevie hadn't brought up anything to do with who she was looking for again, and James didn't ask. He wasn't in the habit of getting into other people's business. When Liza used to fill him in on the latest news and gossip from the people at school, he'd usually blissfully zone out and contribute an irregular 'yes' or 'no way'. Secretly, she knew he wasn't listening, but she'd tell him all the same. That was probably one of the main reasons Liza was so popular, she knew everything about everyone. When you are sixteen, beautiful, and in high school, that's all that's necessary, along with an attractive boyfriend, for people to like you, or probably more accurately, for them to want to be like you.

While none of that appealed to James, he knew the real Liza. She was sensitive and witty and always knew what he was thinking no matter how hard he tried to block everyone out. Other than maybe his mum, she was the only one who could do that. Dating your best friend of over ten years came with its disadvantages and advantages but knowing each other inside out usually fell into the latter.

"It's my mum. The person I'm looking for," Stevie whispered to James as they lay tops and tails on the soft three-seater couch trying to doze off. He still wasn't comfortable with using the bedrooms, and even if he had been, they hadn't managed to find a bed anywhere, so the wide couch was the only comfortable bit of furniture they owned, or more accurately - could use.

"You've never spoken about her before," James whispered back, following her lead and looking up at the ceiling, avoiding eye contact until she was ready.

"My dad, the one who I travel with, the one who I lived with, isn't really my dad. I suppose he's technically my uncle. I've called him dad since I moved in with him when I was six because that's what he feels like to me, but I've never had parents in the traditional sense. I never knew my actual dad, and you could say my mum wasn't the best role model as a kid, so her brother stepped in. I didn't see her after that, not until her funeral a few years later."

James didn't know what to say, his dad rarely said much, and his mum was overbearing at the best of times, but he couldn't imagine growing up without them. He had a feeling Stevie's stories of her extravagant life were exaggerated, but to have no parents... "How do you know she's not in Torpor? We haven't even looked for her here yet, we should have spent the week..."

Before he could finish Stevie interrupted, "She's not in Torpor, she's in Tartarus. If a third of us end up there, she has to be. As I said, she wasn't the best role model when I was a kid, but if you can't drink here I doubt you can in Tartarus, so all that would be left is the good in her, the kind her, the mum that used to make me pancakes and dance with me in the kitchen. She doesn't deserve to be there like that. I need to find her."

The next morning James woke up early to find an eagerly awaiting Stevie standing over him raring to go. "I couldn't sleep, there's just too much happening today," she offered as he stretched out on the couch. James didn't sleep very well either, today was the first day on his journey to the other worlds, and even though he'd scolded Stevie when he thought she wanted to become a Whiteflyer for the powers alone, he couldn't deny he was excited to play with fire, float in the air and find out whatever else it was that they could do. As he saw it, once they didn't encourage and take part in the Whiteflyer's intimidation, there was no reason they couldn't have some fun with it.

Unlike their last visit, this time James and Stevie decided to drive to Trafalgar Square. Most of the cars parked up and down the streets had keys left in them, and because nobody was allowed to own possessions, it was a free for all when it came to which cars they could drive. They'd spent a whole day the week before driving around Torpor looking for cool cars to upgrade to. They'd finished the day with a Jaguar, but to James' dismay it was gone by the time they'd woken up the next morning.

This morning they went with a simple dark blue hatchback, it was for the best that they didn't draw too much attention to themselves right off the bat. Stevie parked the car a couple of streets away and they strolled up a little early to find a good spot before the announcement started. Unfortunately, it wouldn't be as easy as James had originally thought to get a good view. Tens of thousands of people lined the square, spilling out onto the roads. There were nearly five times as many people as the only other time they'd been the week before. It seemed they weren't the only ones excited to see what would happen with the news of the enrolment of more Whiteflyers.

Stevie took the lead, squishing her way through the sardine packed crowd, pulling an awkward James behind her. They settled in a spot near one of the grand fountains, just in time for the bell to go off announcing the arrival of the Whiteflyers. The forty men and women that came last time tripled to over a hundred, all just as eager as the next to show off and intimidate the crowd. The power display with water, fire, air and for a select few earth, continued just as it had on their previous visit. When everyone settled, the same stern woman from the week before began to read out the names of the newcomers to Torpor, she also took Hatt's place this week and gave a brief overview of the rules.

James zoned out as she read aloud, instead taking a more detailed look at some of the Whiteflyers. The woman reading was short and slim and must have been about 65 years old when she died. Her short mousy brown hair reminded James of pictures of his mum from the 80s. She didn't seem like the type of person who would sign up to be a Whiteflyer, but then again, a body's age didn't make a difference to fitness, health or stamina once it died. Anne attested to that more than once to James' everlasting surprise. Her thin frail body could lift things Stevie would even struggle with. This woman did look like the power hungry type, so James imagined her reasoning for becoming a Whiteflyer was for status alone.

Hatt was a good looking man with fair hair that continued onto his face to form a short beard. His body was around 30. *The man from the week before had said Hatt had been here since the 1600's, so maybe that wasn't that young an age to die back then. Suppose that explains why there aren't as many old bodies as you'd expect to find in a world where the dead lived,* James thought to himself, realising for the first time that there may be even more people that had bodies that looked like they had died under the age of 50 than over.

When the woman finished Hatt began to speak and James who was eager to learn more about becoming a Whiteflyer, immediately clued in, "As always, the annual call for Whiteflyers has brought out a substantial number of Torpor residents to witness those who have the guts to compete to become their best selves. Every year, Torpor, along with Tartarus and Arcadius, are asked to produce ten new Whiteflyers to join The Controller to help keep order. Over and over, Tartarus and Arcadius get a dozen times the amount of applications as Torpor, resulting in a poorer, more pathetic pool of candidates for us to choose the successful from. This is even further proof that both the noble and the evil have far higher aspirations than most of you can ever hope to reach. This year, while I don't expect it, I hope you prove me wrong."

Stevie rolled her eyes and cleared her throat a bit too dramatically for James to believe she had something stuck in it, "Maybe they don't apply because they don't want to work for you and your posse of brown nosers," she said under her breath, forcing James to let out a laugh.

Hatt continued, gesturing at the man they'd met in Stevie's, "Everyone who applies will go through two months of intense training with Vask and a select few other Whiteflyers. You will learn to control Fire, Water, Air and Earth. At the end you'll prove your worth and the ten worthiest amongst you will be chosen to join us. However, the unsuccessful will not be allowed to return back to society. For 100 years, they will serve the needs of the Whiteflyers and by extension, The Controller himself. Those looking to apply should do it solely for the chance to serve the Three Worlds, so there is no reason that this should deter anyone from signing up. It is one extra way that even the weak can do their bit to keep order."

Hatt stood back, motioning with his hands for the onlookers to step aside, allowing for a walkway to form in between the crowd. With a simple arm movement, he lifted the ground, creating a narrow catwalk that led towards him. Even some of the other Whiteflyers looked impressed with the ease of his abilities and at how natural the high path looked, like it had always been there. When he finished, Vask stepped forward, "Those looking to apply, make your way to the front."

James and Stevie took a long silent look at each other, the possible 100-year sentence of serving these obnoxious people seemed beyond horrific, but with a nod from James they both jumped onto the platform. There was no other way. Others began to follow and in total around 90 people signed their name, and possible prison sentence. They walked through the doors of the Whiteflyer's headquarters to complete their training. "This is it," Stevie said to James as she came up behind him and squeezed the tops of his arms. "There is no going back."

4. "WELCOME HOME!"

Everyone who had nominated themselves to try to become a Whiteflyer huddled together in the grand entrance of the Whiteflyer's headquarters. The inside of the building was even more spectacular than the outside. It was filled with colour and art, reminding James of everything that Torpor was missing. The entrance was open and spacious, and the domed glass ceiling gave James the impression that the sky was his limit. The richly painted high red walls and the intricate details of the panels and columns surrounding them were in stark contrast to the rest of the places James and Stevie had been to since arriving at Torpor. Not everything on Earth appeared in Torpor and that which was colourful and warming had until now, translated to this world in its most simple and dull form. But not this building, this building was magical.

"Welcome home!" came a familiar voice from the doorway. "Well, for the next two months anyway." As the candidates pulled their eyes away from the grandeur of the hall to find out who was talking, the Whiteflyers who had just come inside began to surround them. When their circle linked at the far end of the room, men and women dressed in full black robes came from the surrounding rooms to leave bowls of water at every second or third Whiteflyer's feet before leaving again. James felt a pang in his stomach as he realised these were the unsuccessful applicants from previous years that were now destined to serve those they had once wished to become.

Together, the Whiteflyers rose a metre in the air and simultaneously roared, "Air". Next, flames covered their floating bodies from head to toe and out came, "Fire". In unison, those with water under their noses directed it to explode onto the awaiting candidates and once more they all screamed, "Water." They finished as Vask, who James now realised was the one to welcome them home and who was leading the chants, raised the centre of the room where the applicants stood with just a move of his hand and one last time the room shouted, "Earth".

"These are the powers you will live, breathe and sleep for the next couple of months. However, by the end of your time here, only the successful will master them" Vask shouted at the dumbstruck recruits. "As the sharpest among you may have noticed, not every Whiteflyer has the ability to use all four powers. This is something that very few people have been able to master in all of the Three Worlds. Powers that you don't have full control over will be taken away from you. Whiteflyer or not, the weak aren't rewarded here. Air and Fire are fourth and third level powers. While they may seem tough to control at first, we haven't yet had to recruit someone who has failed either of those classes. Water is a second level power, just under half of the Whiteflyers in this room can control it, so very few of you will learn to master it. Finally, Earth, a first level, is reserved only for the very best amongst us."

James looked around at the Whiteflyers surrounding him, a few looked ashamed and embarrassed, others remained neutral, and one or two had smug smiles on their faces. He guessed these were the few who had become experts in all four levels. "For now, one of our drudges will take you to your living quarters," Vask continued as one of the men dressed in black re-entered the room. "This will be where you will sleep and socialise for the next two months. Practice begins tomorrow at sunrise. Oh, and before I forget, there are two rules you must obey while you are with us. No skipping practice and no fighting outside of it."

Stevie, James and the other recruits followed the man Vask had labelled a drudge out of the hall. He led them through many more elaborately designed rooms filled with grand furniture that James had only seen before on school trips to museums or on TV. One room, entirely dedicated to music, was decorated with old records, CDs and every type of musical instrument he could think of, and some he never even knew existed before. It made him realise just how much he was missing listening to his favourite songs on the walk home from school, or during his regular visits to the local gym. He and Stevie had looked for a way to play music a few days after they came to Torpor, but their hunt went unrewarded. They had just assumed it wasn't possible until-now. None of the abandoned shop buildings, or even houses they had ventured into, showed any signs that music was something they would be able to listen to anymore.

"Surprise, surprise, there is music in Torpor, but only the elite get access to it. I bet they even watch TV here," Stevie grunted to James, not caring who heard. "Yeah, pretty cool right," a tall muscular girl with blonde hair next to them responded. "Perks of being a Whiteflyer, I guess. Even more reason to put everything I have into becoming the best."

"Yeah because the Whiteflyers we've seen seem like 'the best'," Stevie retorted sarcastically.

Luckily, the girl didn't pick up on her blatant mockery and instead stuck out her pale hand and introduced herself, "I'm Rowena, my friends call me Rowe. I died a few months ago in an unfortunate accident, and I've been bored stiff waiting for my chance to prove myself ever since. It's rather embarrassing that we ended up here, don't you think? The way Hatt seems to see it, even those in Tartarus are better than us. Even if they were not rewarded for it, they had at least made an impact during their lives." Stevie being Stevie avoided the handshake and instead flashed a winning smile, not caring to introduce herself in turn. James grinned to himself and shook his head.

After ten minutes, the recruits arrived at the other side of the building. It wasn't as grand as the rooms they'd first ventured through, but it still had the characteristically high ceilings, hard wood floors and colourfully painted walls. It was only missing the elaborate furniture and famous paintings that covered the rest of the headquarters. Without saying anything, the drudge stopped suddenly outside two double doors. He pulled an old key out of his black robes to unlock them, leading everyone into their home for the next two months.

The first room, down the long empty hall coming from the double doors, was roughly the same size as James' house had been. It was filled with a large gym mat surrounded by benches and stools. The far end of the room had ten target boards pinned to the forest green walls. They looked old and worn out and they were even burnt in places. But it only added to their character and succeeded in getting James even more excited. As a child, he always loved playing with fire. He'd burnt his fingers too many times putting candle flames out with his wet hands. "Cool. It must be our training room," a man in his early 70s stated obviously, as they all took a closer look around. James had overheard him refer to himself as Richie Taylor. He was a slender yet muscular guy that reminded James of an older man he'd often see training at his gym.

The next room down the corridor was half the size of the last and was filled with four sets of four royal red couches. It was somewhere, James presumed, that they could relax between training sessions. Opposite the living room was their bedroom, complete with rows of simple metal bunk beds, the kind you'd find in army barracks. It was obvious by the number of prepared beds, that even though Hatt had said he hoped Torpor's residents proved him wrong and signed up to try and become a Whiteflyer, that he had not prepared for that eventuality. On the left side of the room, a long open wardrobe revealed an array of simple grey clothes that the recruits could use while they trained. The communal garments reminded James of Hatt's first speech that they'd watched, where he forbade the residents from possessing anything. At the time James didn't imagine that rule applied to everything down to his clothes, but nonetheless, he was happy to change out of the dirty ones that he'd been wearing since dressing for brunch the morning he died. Grey loose fit pants, a grey t-shirt and a grey short robe, paired with grey trainers and a grey scrunchy for the girls seemed to be the only daytime outfits available to them. The wardrobe also held two rows of grey nightwear and a large drawer filled with grey underwear that, according to a sign, could also be used for bathing.

The last room at the end of the hall was their bathroom, complete with a bath the size of a small swimming pool and four walls covered in showers. They were the kind that James' local swimming pool had when he went for lessons when he was a kid. They certainly didn't scream privacy. Nothing in his new living quarters did. On entering the bathroom, the recruit's eyes were immediately drawn to the centre, where a huge fountain resided in the middle of the bath. It boasted a tall and strong man, presented as almost godlike. At his feet four circular symbols representing Air, Fire, Water and Earth were carved into the stone. If James was a betting man, he'd put money on it that this was supposed to represent the Controller. Whether it was created in his likeness was yet to be determined. The man in the statue was a lot younger than James had imagined The Controller to be, but people could be vain when it came to things like this.

When the drudge left the recruits to settle into their new temporary abode, Rowe jumped onto the top bunk nearest the door. "Bags," she announced to the room. Everyone else followed suit and Stevie and James settled for two bottom bunks next to each other in the middle of the room.

When two guys in their early to mid-twenties took the beds above them, Stevie, having the outgoing personality James now associated with her, appeared from under the bed to introduce herself, "Hey, I am Stevie Miller and this is James Moore. I guess we will be living beside each other for the next while."

The two looked at each other and smiled. "Well hello there, aren't you the prettiest roommate I've ever had. I'm Matthew, Matthew Avery," said the taller one, jumping down off the bed and moving too close to Stevie for James' liking.

"And I'm Tim Greer," the other guy introduced himself, following his friend and jumping off the bed to stand beside Stevie. Both were staring at her with goggling eyes and sheepish grins. James swore he even saw the second guy, Tim, lick his lips.

He tensed up, ready to put himself between the two guys and Stevie if necessary. He didn't like the look of either of them. They reminded him of the sleazy football players in school that used to flirt with Liza when he wasn't around, sometimes even when he was. He'd gotten suspended for getting in a fight with one of them before. Stevie didn't need protecting like Liza did though, she was well capable of holding her own. "Well I don't know about that," Stevie remarked with a hint of laughter in her tone. "Tim looks very pretty to me. What do you think James?"

"Mm I dunno, I can see what you mean but pretty isn't the word I'd use to describe him," James replied, snorting and pushing his nose up with his finger to mimic Tim's pig snout. Stevie howled with laughter, frustrating Tim even further. His raw red fists bunched up as he launched himself towards a smirking James, only missing his target because Matthew jumped in the way reiterating what Vask had said about fighting outside of practice.

"Watch your back Moore," Tim threatened as Matthew pushed him towards two alternative empty beds near a delighted Rowe.

"So, that keeps the total number of people I'd trust not to knife me in the back at the first chance they'd get, at one, and I still have my reservations about you," Stevie joked to James as she lay down on top of her bed.

"Doesn't bother me. I wouldn't trust anyone from here to help us either way," James told her. "Did you really think the Whiteflyer wannabes would be any better than the Whiteflyers themselves?"

Stevie was quiet for a minute in thought before responding, "Yeah I guess not. Maybe we should at least pretend to fit in though. I can't imagine we will be chosen if Vask or anyone else finds out the real reason we're here and I, for one, don't want to end up a drudge. Did you notice they don't even talk? What's that about?" James shrugged, he wasn't going to become a drudge, that's the last thing he'd let happen. This was his best chance of finding Liza, and he wasn't going to give Tim, Matthew or anyone else a chance to stop that from happening.

After a couple of hours lounging around the living quarters and getting to know the different recruits, James was more sure than ever that he despised Matthew and Tim. The two of them, along with Rowe, had spent the afternoon trying their best to intimidate the other recruits and make themselves out to be shoe-ins to take three of the ten Whiteflyer places. It became apparent that Matthew had a long line of relations that had succeeded and became Whiteflyers in all three worlds. Their family were legends of sorts in the Three Worlds. His Grandad and Great Grandmother had both gone on to become Whiteflyers after they arrived in Torpor. He had even spent the afternoon bragging to anyone who would listen that his Grandad now held three of the four powers and his Great Grandmother held all four. She was the woman, who Stevie and James now knew as Catherine Avery, who had addressed the Torpor residents with Hatt and Vask. Apparently she would be teaching them about the history of the universe. The real history that the people on Earth were oblivious to. Her portrait hung in their training room along with seven other people, including Hatt and Vask. They were the only eight people from Torpor who wielded all four powers. They were supposed to be a constant reminder and motivation to all of the recruits as to what their end goal should be.

A few of the other recruits really clung to the rubbish Matthew, Tim and Rowe were spouting and congregated into a little fan group around them. It reminded James of Liza and her friends in school. *She wasn't anything like these three though, she got attention, but she didn't need it, people were just naturally drawn to her,* James reminded himself as he watched Matthew attempt to flirt with a particularly pretty chocolate brown haired girl named Tessa. James couldn't imagine Tessa would have shown any interest in Matthew back on Earth, but the stories about his powerful family seemed to be doing the trick. Maybe she thought Catherine Avery would decide in her favour if she was dating her great grandson, or maybe she was just conceited and was turned on by status and influence.

Out of those that didn't think sucking up to Matthew and his posse was necessary to become a Whiteflyer, James and Stevie got on with Richard, or Richie as he liked to be called, the best. It seemed odd that someone of his age and kind nature would sign himself up for something like this, healthy body or not, but after talking to him, James began to understand his reasoning, "After being here for as long as I have, you quickly realise there's only so much you can do to occupy your time. On Earth I was always on the tennis court or picking up my grandkids from school. I am a busy body at heart. When I realised my kids weren't going to join me, I decided that it was time for my next adventure. Who knows how far I'll go, but if the next two months of training go nowhere, I'll at least have the memories to keep me going."

After a while, Stevie and James grew restless hanging around and waiting for the following day to arrive. They yearned to begin training and finally get a better idea of what they were in for, for the next two months, which would hopefully turn into forever. Stevie proposed exploring the rest of the headquarters at one point, but the double doors proved to be locked from the outside. James guessed that leaving the recruits area was another rule that Vask had forgotten to mention, or maybe he just didn't see the point when the doors would be locked anyway. Sitting in the living area, they decided to join two of the other recruits, Annabelle and Marcus, for a long swim before an early night, but as they got up to get changed, James heard the double doors creak open in the hall next to them.

In walked a Whiteflyer they hadn't spoken to before, but one that James had noticed during the display earlier that day in the entrance hall. She had a young memorable face that could pull off her shortly cut blonde hair. She was one of the nonchalant looking Whiteflyers that he witnessed mastering three of the four powers. However, she wasn't one of the seven hanging on the wall of the training room, so he assumed she hadn't managed to hold onto the final one, Earth.

Behind the woman stood six drudges, dressed in their usual black, all holding silver trays stacked with needles and empty vials, each marked with a name. "I hope nobody is scared off just yet, it is only day one after all, and that's only if you choose to count the day before training begins. I am Elizabeth Clark, my best friends call me Lizzy, which none of you are by the way. Not yet anyway." At that last part Rowe smiled, and James could see into her fantasies about becoming a Whiteflyer and being accepted into the pack. He then looked at Stevie and couldn't help but smile at the contrast. Her face looked like she'd stood in poo. For the first time, he realised just how different she was to Liza. While he didn't think Liza would approve of the Whiteflyers, Rowes' eagerness to impress Elizabeth reminded him of the girls in school who looked up to his girlfriend. Stevie on the other hand was super friendly and outgoing but she didn't care for social status or false pretences of being cool. He imagined she wouldn't have been in the popular group at school. University would have been more her scene when it came to making friends, from what he'd heard from Jen anyway, it wasn't supposed to be as cliquey.

Coming back to the room, for the first time James carefully eyed the long needles that the drudges held. They were empty, proving they were for extraction, not for injection. "I need six lines of fifteen. Hatt has asked for your blood," Elizabeth gestured to the room, but to no response. "Now!", she clicked at the dumb struck recruits. "If you're scared of a needle you may as well hand in your grey robes for black ones before the sun comes up. The Controller has no time for cowards." At this the room quickly did as they were told. Six by six they stepped up and let the drudges take a vial of their blood.

5. "I NEED A VOLUNTEER."

The following morning, the ninety recruits were harshly awoken a little before sunrise to the chiming of a large brass bell. With no windows, it was impossible to tell where the sounds were coming from, but it was not unlike the bell that had rung before the Whiteflyers addressed Torpor. It was, however, quieter and something told James it was for the recruits benefit alone and he'd better get used to waking up to it. Sleeping with one eye on Stevie, after their run-in with Matthew and Tim, James could have done with another hour or two of rest before he had to get up and begin the most important day of his existence so far. However, the excitement of starting to train with superpowers of a sort was enough to get him up, dressed, and ready before the double doors were unlocked.

Into the living area came a drudge, the same one that had led them to their living quarters the day before, and for the first time, he spoke, "If everyone can line up in pairs I can bring you to the outside training grounds." The chatter that filled the common area the night before had faded out, and excitedly, with a hint of anxiety for fear of the unknown, the recruits obeyed. Out the doors they turned left, through more of the building they had still not yet explored. Once again, they were brought through grand corridors and fancily furnished rooms. James' eyes still lit up at the sight of them. Stevie was a lot more relaxed and barely seemed to notice the splendour of it all. Whether this was due to her rich upbringing or lack of materialism, James wasn't sure. After two more rooms, they arrived at a large archway leading outside.

If their indoor training room had impressed them the day before, it was nothing after seeing the grounds in front of them. A large oval, the size of a soccer field, surrounded by high walls, was filled with everything needed to master the four powers. The quarter to their immediate left was empty, save for the ground of sand most likely used to soften their fall as they learned to control Air and a row of boxes filled with items that they would at some point have to float and manipulate to do as they pleased. The box closest, and the only one open, held single stem flowers. The section above Air's training quarter had a gravel ground that was surrounded by target boards, not unlike the burnt ones inside. The far side of this area held sprinklers, fire blankets and extinguishers. To the far right of the training ground, a deep swimming pool with walkways spinning through it was where they were to learn the ways of Water. And lastly, and most arduously, was Earth's training area. This quarter of the oval had a flat ground sectioned into multiple areas, all made out of a different material. James could now see why Earth was such a difficult power to master. With so many natural elements to manipulate, it was nearly like learning 25 powers in one.

Unmissably, in between everything, stood seventeen Whiteflyers, with Catherine and Vask front and centre. "Yesterday, I told you that that was your home," Vask said, pointing to the headquarters behind them. His voice, like Hatt's and Catherine's had previously, travelling an eerily far distance. "I spoke too soon. This is your real home. This training ground is the only place you should be thinking about for the next two months. When you are talking, sleeping, bathing and dressing, this is the only place, thing, or person that needs to be on your mind. Fantasising about becoming a Whiteflyer two months from now won't get you there. Being 100% present during training and going over and meticulously planning and executing your next day of training afterwards will.

"For three quarters of your waking day, I will be your boyfriend, your dad, your brother. For one class a week, Catherine Avery will take you for history. The other parts should, and will, be spent memorising, practicing and mastering what you've learnt from both of us. At the end of the two months, you will go up against yourselves and each other in front of every Torpor Whiteflyer. All of who have been through what you will, all who have defied the odds and made something of themselves. Only the most outstanding ten will get to keep their powers after that. You have already been told what will happen to the rest of you."

When Vask finished, each of the Whiteflyers lined up and introduced themselves. These were the recruit's trainers, each of them specialising in a certain power. When Catherine stood forward, to James' inner annoyance, she made reference to her long lineage of Whiteflyer family members, mentioning Matthew as the next talented Avery she was hopeful would prove himself and make the cut. Stevie's displeasure wasn't as secretive as James' and her snort drew the attention of a snide Rowe next to her, "Jealous much? I can imagine you come from a family of lazy and filthy swines."

James watched as Stevie's face grew red and her hands clasped but thankfully, before she could respond, a handful of drudges distractingly spilled out into the training ground. Each of them holding a rack of vials containing the blood the recruits had sacrificed the night before. As they lined up Vask began to talk again, "As you should know by now, none of you are currently worthy enough to meet The Controller in person. Your vials of blood were brought to him last night to temporarily grant you powers. Those powers are on loan, they do not belong to you. Even those successful enough to become Whiteflyers are only given powers for as long as The Controller wishes it. They are given to you to do his bidding and his bidding only. This is not for selfish or vain reasons, but for the protection of the Three Worlds. You will find out more about this during your time with Catherine."

When Vask finished he nodded to the drudge in the middle, who was standing one step closer to the Whiteflyers than the others, to begin the process. She had the oldest body James had seen since he'd been in the headquarters. It was a woman of a similar age to Anne, the woman living in his house. Even though some of the other drudges may have been older in years but not in body, it still saddened him to see her amongst them. "When your name is called please step forward and retrieve your vial." The drudge went down the list of names in alphabetical order, ticking them off like his school teachers used to do to make sure they were all in class, "Matthew Avery, Lily Barnes, Marcus Davis......Stevie Miller, James Moore.....", and in turn the recruits stepped forward and retreated back, impatiently waiting until all 90 names were called so they could hurry up and start using their powers.

Casually, as if it was the only logical next step, Vask stepped forward to explain, "Now that everyone has been accounted for and has retrieved their blood. Please remove the stopper and drink it back in one gulp." When they looked at each other confused he continued, "Does that unnerve some of you? It is your own blood. It was in your body yesterday, there's no reason it can't go back today."

James was one of the first to go for it. He threw the vial back down his throat and waited for some sort of surge of energy, for something that would let him know that it worked. Just as he started to think the Whiteflyers were playing a cruel trick on the unsuspecting recruits, he began to feel a slight tingle travelling up his body from his toes. His skin felt electric, but not uncomfortable or unfamiliar, it was like a huge part of him was missing and it had finally come home.

"Wow, cool," Tim exclaimed animatedly to the onlooking Whiteflyers, who were eagerly waiting to see how the recruits would react. "I need to release it. I can feel it inside me. It's building up. I need to..." but before he finished his sentence a wisp of air came gushing forward from where the Whiteflyers stood, knocking him onto his back.

"You need to do nothing!" Vask roared at Tim and then at the rest of them when they laughed at his mishap. "Controlling your powers is the most important element to learn if you want to master them. Any idiot can be given powers and figure out how to make something happen. It's when you match your powers to your mind that we will see who the real Whiteflyers are amongst you."

After a long pause, and when a much redder Tim had returned to his feet, four of the Whiteflyers, including Elizabeth who they'd met the night before, stepped forward and ushered them towards the bottom left quarter of the oval to begin their first lesson of their training, Air.

Split into four groups, the recruits lined up waiting for their initial instructions. Stevie and James were unfortunately stuck in a group with Matthew and Tim. Their instructor was a young man who had introduced himself to them as Bill Watson, but who they were asked to just address as Watson. He was a blonde and strong looking man who had explained that he had been in Torpor since the mid 1800's when he first introduced himself. "I need a volunteer." Both Matthew and James shot forward, waving their hand in the air, eager to learn more and more importantly to get chosen over the other person. "Moore is it? Let's see what you have got," Watson addressed James, to an openly pissed off Matthew's dismay.

"Right! Listen to me very carefully and remove any preconceptions that you have about how your powers work. Close your eyes and concentrate closely on the tingling feeling moving up, down, and around your body." James obeyed taking in everything Watson was saying, reminding himself that he needed to prove himself if he wanted to find Liza. "Feel the air, no matter how light, brushing past you. Picture it going through your hair and ruffling your clothes." As he said this James could feel the wind get slightly more intense in those areas. He guessed Watson had something to do with that. He was using his powers to help James draw on his. The Whiteflyer stepped forward, placing a single flower into James' outstretched hand. "Move it," he demanded. "Control the tingle to move as you please it. Match it to the air you can feel surrounding you. Bring them together and move the flower." James tried for what felt like two minutes and then ten and then twenty, but nothing happened. He was about to give up until he heard faint laughter behind him. No prizes for guessing who it was coming from. He wouldn't give them the satisfaction.

"You're not clearing your mind. You're not solely concentrating on the task at hand. At this moment, nothing else is important." James did as he was told. He forgot about the sniggering noises coming from an elated Matthew and a few of his followers. He forgot about why he was here. He forgot about Liza. He concentrated all of his everything on moving the tingle around his body to meet the air he could feel swishing past his robes, tickling his skin, and sending a chill up his spine. And in that instant, that his mind blanked out everything else completely, the flower moved.

"Bravo!" Watson clapped, retrieving the fallen flower and handing it back to James. "It usually takes people most of the day to do that for the first time." Pointing at the basket of flowers to his right, he then addressed the rest of his group, "Now the rest of you, let's see if you find it as funny when you are put in the hot seat."

The recruits spent the rest of the day practicing blowing the flowers to the ground. Watson moved between them, magnifying the wind so they could connect to it easier. Even though James had done it once, it still took a lot of concentration and effort, especially when Watson was no longer intensifying the wind around him. He forced himself to do it again and again until it was almost second nature. To James' amusement, it took Matthew half the day to make his flower move, and the other half of the day to make it move every time he tried. He wasn't so smug anymore watching James do it over and over. Tim was completely useless and at one point Watson even asked him if he was all talk and no brain.

Unfortunately, by the end of the first day of training Stevie didn't prove to be much better than Tim and had only just managed to make hers move once or twice. James had tried to help her at one point, but Vask who was observing from a stone chair he'd manifested from the ground, jumped down and put a stop to it before he was able to, "In case it wasn't clear Moore, only ten out of the ninety odd of you will be chosen. Everyone, even your little girlfriend here, is your competition. Helping each other out can be seen to some of the Whiteflyers, including me, as a sign of weakness or lack of dedication to being chosen." After that, James didn't chat to Stevie much for the rest of training and in contrast to what Vask probably thought, it wasn't because of the reminder that Stevie was his competition, because he didn't see it that way. As far as he was concerned, they were in it together. It was Stevie being called his girlfriend that had made him feel awkward and even somewhat guilty. She was only a friend, Liza was his girlfriend, and she could be anywhere, even Tartarus, while he was here making other people assume that him and Stevie were going out. He told himself this one too many times as he went through the motions connecting the tingle and the air.

When the same bell that had woken them up that morning chimed, Vask announced that the first day of training had come to an end and motioned for the four groups to come back together for a debriefing. Watson along with the three other leading Whiteflyers rated the people in their groups from best to worst aloud. Vask claimed that this was for his own information but to do it so publicly, so the other recruits were made aware of where each person stood, could only have one benefit and that was to increase the level of competition in the group. James smiled as his name was read out first in his group. He even got a head nod from Vask, but his pride quickly turned into a pang of guilt as Stevie's name was read fifth to last. They'd never talked about it, but what if only one of them got through? Would he leave Stevie to become a drudge alone? Would he allow her to become a menial servant of the Whiteflyers as he went exploring the other worlds?

After they were escorted back to their living quarters, Stevie, not for the first time since he'd met her, turned to James as if she could read his mind, "I wouldn't expect you to forfeit being a Whiteflyer if I didn't make it. However, that won't be something you'll have to decide. It's day one. Do you really think I'd give Rowena the satisfaction of getting to keep her powers without me?" She smiled and outstretched her arms to mimic a flying motion, her grey robe in hand. "I have always fancied myself a superhero of sorts."

James smiled back realising she was right, it was only the beginning of their training. He shouldn't let rankings and Whiteflyer mind games get to his head. For all he knew, he could be far worse than her at Fire or Water, or even at Air by the end of the two months. "I wouldn't expect anything less Ms Miller."

Even though the recruits, and not even all of them, had only learnt to control enough wind to push a flower off their palm, the rest of the evening was spent enthusiastically going over what had happened that day. They still weren't completely used to the newly found tingle that ran through their skin and it only served to heighten their excitement. As they crowded around the common room couches, the four groups shared stories of who made the best and worst impressions on their team leaders, and even Matthew and his posse found it hard to suppress their laughter when Stevie shared Watson's comments about Tim.

That night, James stayed awake later than his sleepy morning self would have thought. Amongst the heavy breathing and the snores surrounding him, he was replaying his day five times and then ten times over in his brain. Just had Vask had demanded of them, he was looking to discover new ways of doing better. Looking at how he could have improved and what he would do differently the next day. With only one day of training, he wasn't yet able to practice without a teacher in their indoor training room, but thinking through the processes got him pumped and ready for anything that could be thrown at him, and even more importantly, it got his mind off Liza and Stevie.

The days were beginning to stretch into weeks since James had crashed his mum's car on the way to brunch with Liza and the longer he went without answers to her whereabouts, the guiltier he was beginning to feel. Vask's throwaway comment about Stevie being his girlfriend irritated him more than it should have done and he didn't know why. What if he was leading Stevie on and they didn't have the same idea in mind for their relationship? What would Liza think about him becoming so close to another girl? And Stevie wasn't bad looking, if anything most people would have found her very attractive, but he didn't think of her that way, she was just his friend. If he'd met her on Earth, he wasn't even sure they'd be friends. In a lot of ways, they were completely different, but then again, in other ways, they were very much the same.

"You awake?", Stevie whispered to James from the bottom bunk next to him.

"Yeah. Just going over today, seeing what I can do better tomorrow."

"Haha, of course you are. I'm playing my favourite Oasis' songs in my head, pretending I have my earphones in and blocking out the fact I'm in a room with nearly one hundred almost strangers. You can stay though." James remained silent. "I was also thinking that we should probably remove the awkward elephant in the room so we can go back to being friends. I don't think another day with a moody quiet James is good for mine or for your training," she teased.

"That obvious?" James asked, happy the light was turned off so Stevie couldn't see the crimson colour rising up into his cheeks.

"Just as obvious as how vexed Matthew was that you were rated first in our group. Why are you listening to them? The Whiteflyers are trying to make us angry, to cut us off from anything that might threaten their end goal, which is to create brainwashed followers to add to their wolf pack. You shouldn't rise to it. I haven't met one of them that even might have our best interests in mind. If we do well in training it reflects well on them, and the same goes in reverse if we do badly. At this point they don't care about anything else. We need to think about what's best for us, not for them." James agreed that the Whiteflyers definitely didn't care about him or any of the other recruits, but maybe concentrating solely on training would cement his place as a Whiteflyer. It was how he'd made that first flower move after all. However, on the other hand, would he just be turning into one of them as he achieved it? He shook his head, angry at himself for letting his thought process go there. That was not the person that Liza loved. Stevie was right, if James wanted to come out of this as the same person he went in as, he needed friends, or at least one. Someone he could confide in. He was sure Liza wouldn't deny him that.

When James didn't reply, too busy with his own thoughts, Stevie continued on the same path, "I'm not trying to replace her James. It's not like that for me and you. We're friends, nothing more, nothing less. Trust me Moore, if I was interested in you like that you would know about it. And anyway, who says you could even get a Stevie Miller? All your flower stem moving today is really going to your head. Next you'll tell me you're friends with Matthew and Tim," Stevie laughed and James' cheeks grew even redder. He was worrying for nothing, he shouldn't have let Vask' comments put words in Stevie's mouth.

"I do sound pretty sure of myself when you put it like that," James replied light heartedly, brushing off his embarrassment. "It's not easy being modest when you're top of the class, as well as tall, dark and handsome."

6. "IT WAS CALLED PERSAVIUS."

On the second day of training, James woke up naturally before the morning bell rang. He decided to start the day off with a hot sudsy bath before anyone else got up. Because clocks and watches didn't work in Torpor, the residents made a rough estimate of the time using the sun. He and Stevie were both useless at it, but Anne would usually put them at ease with her fairly accurate guesses whenever they bumped into her. Nevertheless, James' skills couldn't be put to the test that morning as the recruit's living quarters didn't even have a window to estimate from. Instead, James hurried and got changed in case his mental clock was completely off and he missed his chance for some alone time. He had already realised that solitude was going to be hard to come by until his training was over. Maybe even longer than that. He knew that Vask didn't live in the Whiteflyer's headquarters because they'd found him at Stevie's old house, but he couldn't be sure if it was the same with everyone. Who knew how long he'd be living with all of these people?

As James melted into the hot bubbly water, his mind went to other places and he allowed himself to fondly remember his first kiss with

Liza. It was before they'd started dating. They were just about to start year 12, so Liza and her friends decided to mourn their discontinued freedom by throwing an end of summer party on their school grounds before it reopened. James' parents had let him drink alcohol once or twice under their supervision, but never more than two or three small beers, so he'd sneakily replaced some of their harder stuff with water for the occasion. He even took some for Liza, who had run out of bottles to nick from her own house. She had drunk a lot more than he had over the summer, spending at least one night a week at a friend's house party or sneaking into some of the local bars using her older cousin's ID. While James liked to drink the odd time, he wasn't as much of a party animal as she was. And if truth be told, he found a lot of her friends to be on the obnoxious side, so he would only join them for special occasions when he was sure more of the class would be there.

That night in the field beside their school's gymnasium, Liza was paying a lot more attention to James than he was used to. He had usually spent most of those nights chatting with his friends Carl and Luke, while she would spend them with her girlfriends, or with Dan, the guy she was casually seeing at the beginning of the summer. James wasn't sure what had happened with them, but one day she just stopped mentioning him. She and Dan didn't talk together anymore when they all met, but they didn't actively argue either. This night, however, Liza didn't move from James' side. They spent hours laughing and playing as if there was nobody else there. Even when the police came to break up the gathering, which they often did when they got a tipoff about underaged kids drinking, James and Liza stuck together. Instead of running off, Liza pulled him into the infamous "smoking bush". A passer-by wouldn't give the bush a second glance, but it was a secret place that was accessible to everyone in the know. Most often, it was used by the kids who smoked at school.

It was there, with a branch sticking into James' back and a wet patch growing on his trousers from sitting on the damp mud, that Liza first told James that she had feelings for him. And, even though he had never before had those feelings himself, he kissed her. He didn't know if it was the alcohol or the adrenaline that made him kiss her, but it surely felt good and, until a week or two ago, he hadn't stopped kissing her ever since.

James was brought back to reality by the sound of the morning bell. Slowly, the recruits piled into the bathroom to wash, disrupting his memories from what felt like a lifetime ago.

"There you are," Stevie gushed as she walked through the doorway. "I thought someone might have kidnapped you while we were sleeping and I'm not going to lie, I wasn't that sad about it. One less person I will have to beat to become a Whiteflyer," she teased, smiling from ear to ear.

"Nope, still here. Your snoring just got too much. I thought I'd err on the safe side of things and evacuate the room in case the whole thing came down," James replied happily.

Stevie's face quickly changed from its previously smug look to one of outrage, "Well, I never! In all my sixteen years of being alive, and my week and a half of being dead…. Ladies do not snore!" And with an upturned head, off she went straight to the shower. James smirked as he pulled himself out of the bath to get ready for his second day.

For the second day, the recruits were split into four groups. James stood next to Stevie purposely, to ensure they'd be allocated to the same group. He wanted to make up for his cold mood with her yesterday by helping her out in training today. Once she had gotten the hang of it, he was confident she'd fly, quite literally, past the rest of the trainees. As luck would have it, Tim, Matthew and Rowe were assigned to a different group and Vask was the furthest away from Stevie and James' group as he could have been. In James' opinion it was the perfect setup to get Stevie moving up the ladder.

Today, James, along with a few other people in the class who were progressing quickly, was given a tennis ball to practice his newfound powers with. His goal was to move the ball through a hoop a metre in front of him. It was the kind of hoop James used to watch his sister Jen move around her body in the garden. He was cocky at first and made a terrible first impression on their teacher, a chubby man whose body was in its late 50s that went by the name of Luca. James found it effortless to compel the ball to float, but the further it got from his body the more detached it felt. It had been half the day and it still hadn't got near the blue plastic hoop and even the fact that nobody else's had either didn't soften the blow to James' ego.

Stevie was once again given a flower. She still had work to do before she could advance further. However, with James' help and instruction she was finding it a lot easier than the day before. Luca wasn't a very strict teacher and didn't mind if there was chatting amongst them, making it easier for James to give her direction. They had gotten to the root of her problem early on that day which gave her something to work on. Being such a chatterbox and an over thinker, clearing her head didn't come easily to Stevie, but when she did manage it, the flower moved even further than James' ball ever did.

Halfway through the day, Vask called for a short break before he explained what would be happening for the second half. It would still be Air related because they had already been told that the first week would have an Air focus, the second a Fire, the third Water, and the last Earth. During the second month, the days would be mixed once they'd learned the basics of each power. James and Stevie sat with Marcus, Annabelle, Richie and one or two others while most of the rest huddled around Matthew. He had gotten the ball through the hoop just before their break and was giving them all a loud run through of how he did it. James could see him eyeing him up as he explained, so he purposely didn't give him the satisfaction of letting him know he could hear.

"Right. Everybody gather around!" Vask shouted, interrupting Tim who had by now taken the stage from Matthew with a dramatic display of how he had died back on Earth. By his account, he had died trying to save his elderly neighbour's dog from their house fire. Marcus had already loudly called bullshit. He had heard Tim tell Matthew the day before that he was asleep when it happened, but that didn't stop Tessa and the other girls gushing about how brave he must be. "For the remainder of the day, I will need everybody back in their groups for the first of many competitions. Each player will score points for their team by putting their new powers to the test. The group that scores the most points will get bragging rights and a two hour slot to watch a movie in the headquarters' cinema room tonight." Loud buzzing excitement erupted and once everyone calmed down Rowena was called up to demonstrate her progress.

She'd moved onto practicing on a tennis ball earlier that day but decided against attempting to make it go through the hoop and instead left it hovering above her hand. Vask and the other Whiteflyers awarded her six points. After twenty or so more people went, it was Stevie's turn. Two of the teams, including James and Stevie's, were pretty close for points at the top of the leader board, but there were still 70 people to go, so it could still be anybody's game. Stevie stepped forward and did the unexpected, surprising even James. She used her powers to remove the loose grey scrunchy in her hair and drop it to her hand. As it was attached to her hair and was light, it wouldn't have been that hard to do, yet it showed imagination. She was the first person to use something other than the flower or tennis ball, and so she was awarded eight points.

With only five more people left, Matthew was up, with James on the side-lines ready to go next. He predictably went straight for the tennis ball, striving to repeat his actions from before the break. However, unlike last time, the ball fell straight to the ground as soon as it moved more than a few inches from his hand. Some of the recruits began to laugh but Matthew took no notice determined to not lose concentration. Picking up the ball, he tried again, desperately trying to prove himself. Once again, the ball dropped, only making it less than halfway to its destination. Embarrassed and confused Matthew went for a third attempt before Vask intervened, "That is enough of that. Three points." To Matthew's shock, Vask then turned his head towards a smiling James on the side-lines, "Very clever Moore. Nine points, which seems to put your team in the lead."

Matthew looked shocked, "James gets nine? He hasn't even..." but before he finished, he realised what the sniggering recruits had been laughing at after his first attempt at getting the ball into the hoop. Matthew turned towards James, his face red and his hands clenched, "You. You were intervening. You were forcing my ball to drop."

James immediately went on the defence. He tensed up, ready for anything Matthew threw at him. But before anything could happen Watson stepped forward, "Stand down Matthew. You were beaten. Deal with it by beating him with your powers next time, instead of resorting to your fists."

Matthew's eyes shifted, possibly deciding whether or not he could throw a punch at James without disobeying an order. With no resolution, he took a long breath and lowered his fists. After the last three people went, James' group were announced as the winners and he and Stevie re-entered their living quarters feeling more positive about their situation than they had since they'd gotten to Torpor.

Later that evening, a drudge brought James, Stevie and the rest of their group to a big windowless room in the basement. It housed a huge screen, the size you'd find in a small cinema room, and thirty to forty enormous brown leather lounge chairs. Stevie and James took a place in the middle, before settling in for a night of familiarity amongst the madness they'd been living in since discovering their new norm. The movie of choice was an old western starring Clint Eastwood. It wouldn't have been James' first choice in film on Earth, but it was surprisingly entertaining. At one point during the evening, a drudge even brought out bags of popcorn for the recruits, shutting down the idea that they couldn't eat in Torpor. They just didn't have to. "One more thing to add to the list of what Whiteflyers can do that the rest of the residents are deprived of," Stevie whispered under her breath before hypocritically grabbing a big handful of the salty balls and shoving them into her mouth.

Three quarters of the way through the movie James noticed as Stevie's eyes started to weigh heavily and she struggled to stay awake. Her head gradually sloped towards James' shoulder, splitting his mind in two. One part of him craved some sort of human touch and he was happy for her to rest on him, but another secretly knew that he wouldn't be pleased if Liza fell asleep on another guy. Alas, he pushed the latter to the back of his brain and persuaded himself that it was nothing. He even convinced himself that it was completely normal to find Stevie drooling on him amusing and somewhat endearing, instead of the disgust he would have had if it was coming from someone like Jen.

When the movie ended, the same drudge who had brought them in to watch the movie, re-entered the room to escort them back. James guessed that he was forbidden from watching the film with them and, not for the first time, he swore to himself that he'd find a way to put an end to the injustice in Torpor. However, before he could even begin to plan how to do that though, he needed to find Liza and he needed to establish himself as one of the more powerful Whiteflyers.

Coming back to the headquarters, James immediately felt a sense of unease. Neither Matthew nor Tim were making any sly or nasty comments about the competition earlier that day and if they were the kind of people that he knew them to be, they wouldn't take too well to their group losing because of his interference. Even when Richie told the other recruits that they'd dined on popcorn, they stayed silent. When he voiced his concerns to Stevie, she told him he was overthinking the situation, "They've lost and they know it. There's nothing they can do about it. It's like Watson told Matthew, he will just have to get you back in practice another time. Vask only has two rules and they're not going to throw away the chance of becoming a Whiteflyer just so they can give you a black eye."

What Stevie had said made sense, but the more James got to know both Matthew and Tim, the more he realised that the only reason they weren't in Tartarus was because they hadn't lived long enough to show Earth their true colours. They didn't seem like the kind of people who decided on their actions through reason, but as far as he could tell they hadn't done anything to him. He half expected his mattress to be missing when he called it a night and walked into the bedroom, but all of his stuff was where he'd left it. That night, James dozed off quicker than usual, the movie from that evening replaying over again in his head.

James took a sharp breath and struggled to jump to a sitting position. Something, or more accurately someone, had gotten hold of his wrists and his ankles. A heavy set of hands pushed down on his chest. The room was pitch black, save for the dim light coming from the hallway. He couldn't see who had gotten hold of him, but it didn't take long to figure it out. He was reefed off the bed as his captors moved towards the door. He could hear Stevie shouting at them to let him go, but it was falling on deaf ears. As James was carried into the lit hallway his suspicions were proven to be facts. Matthew had hold of his arms, Tim his legs. Another guy, Rufus, who he'd never so much as had a one on one conversation with, held his torso. James quickly moved his head from left to right, trying to gather his bearings and stay a step ahead of them. As far as he could tell, he was being brought to the bathroom.

"You're not laughing anymore are you, Moore? If you think you're going to beat me ever again by cheating, you can think again," Matthew spat.

James forced a grin on his face, refusing to let them think he was beaten. "It's okay to feel threatened, Avery. I know I would if I were you. All of your family members are top of the class, yet poor Matthew doesn't even realise when his powers are being intercepted." James, eager to keep talking, to distract them, turned to Tim, "And don't even get me started on you…" but before he could get his words out, he found himself falling face down into the bath.

He could feel the water enter his throat and he desperately tried to gain enough control to free his lungs from their upcoming fate. He only managed a second of breath before a hand clasped onto his hair and pushed his head under again. But that second of air gave him enough energy to prepare for his next window. He clenched his fist and readied his arm, breaking through the top of the water and launching his fist at whoever had hold of his head. He opened his eyes just in time to see Tim collapse backwards. Matthew and Rufus lunged forward to stop James from getting out of the bath, but Tim's falling body was blocking their way. James jumped out of the bath, readying himself for the inevitable showdown.

Just then, Marcus and a few of the other recruits made their way into the bathroom, crashing through the chair that was obstructing their path. They grabbed Matthew and Rufus, pulling them into the hallway. Marcus turned towards James, putting his body in the way of any possible retaliation. It was over.

Over the next couple of days, nobody brought up what had happened that morning. Vask drilled the recruits on what had happened to Tim's face when he came to training with a red eye, but nobody in the class caved and ratted anybody out. Even when he made them run rings around the training court for half the morning, they adamantly stuck to Tim's story about falling out of bed. Vask had eventually forgotten about it and come to the conclusion that Tim was just that clumsy. It wasn't completely unbelievable after all. While some of the other recruits would have loved to get rid of both Matthew and James, who were nearly always outperforming the rest of the class, they didn't want to risk getting on the bad side of Tim and Matthew if telling Vask about the fight wasn't enough to get them disqualified.

By now, the recruits had been taught how to use air to move small and medium objects. James' power radius was currently 20 metres. Fifty metres was where he needed to get to if he wanted to be considered to have mastered the power. Well, the distance part of it anyway. The weight, type of object, speed and the obstacles in the way were just as important. Stevie had made huge progress in their four days of practice, she had made her way to the top third of people in the rankings. While this still wasn't good enough to get picked for a Whiteflyer position and even though she still had a long way to go, if she improved at this pace, she would make it no problem. Her nighttime meditation was helping her to calm her mind when she needed to.

On their fifth morning of training, a drudge collected the recruits from their living quarters as usual but unlike the other mornings, he took a right turn instead of the usual left towards the training grounds. They arrived at a grand mahogany staircase, and then another, until they reached the highest room in the building. Inside, rows of desks littered the floor with three high bookshelves pinned to all of the walls bar one. This wall was reserved for a vast open window overlooking London. At the head of the room, Catherine Avery sat waiting to begin their first history lesson.

James and Stevie had briefly wondered when they'd be meeting Catherine again, but the pressure of their practical training always pushed the thought from their minds. James was never great in school so he assumed the same would be the case for Torpor's history lessons. He'd always managed to maintain a high C, low B average, but even that was usually down to Liza's instruction. She was one of those natural brainiacs that didn't have to put much effort in yet always came out with an A.

"Take your seats, recruits. I've only got you for one morning a week and we've got a lot to get through. The Three Worlds history is a lot more complex than anything you've learnt before," Catherine announced, motioning to the recruits to sit down. "Even though The Controller permits people to have an education while they are on Earth, the history, religion, geography and science lessons are in a lot of ways useless here. Half of what is taught is fiction while the other half is relevant to Earth alone. However, that education does a good job of helping to steer lives. For example, it teaches people the error of human ways and the way they react is monitored. Earth education plays its part in shaping the path people take in life. That path ultimately decides which world they are destined for. For Example, Rowena Daley is it?" Catherine addressed Rowe.

"Yes, but most people just call me Rowe," Rowe replied brightly, chuffed to be the one chosen out of everyone.

"Did finding out how damaging plastic is to Earth, force you to think twice about using it Rowena?" Catherine asked, ignoring Rowe's request to use colloquial terms. Rowe stayed silent and grew bright red. James covered his mouth quickly trying not to let a laugh escape. The thought of Rowe sitting at home organising her recycling by material was too much.

"Yes that's what I thought, but I'd imagine if the same question was asked in Arcadius the answer would be very different," Catherine added, before pointing at five people from the front row, and then to a stack of books piled up at the front of her desk, "You five, start handing these out." To Matthew's annoyance he was one of the ones chosen. Catherine had mentioned him on their first morning of training, but she hadn't seemed to take an interest since then. She didn't so much as nod back at him when he greeted her on entrance to the room.

"Ha. I guess she isn't going to play favourites after all. I bet she hadn't met him properly when she was introducing him as her great grandchild the other day. I know I wouldn't be too pleased if he was part of my bloodline," Stevie observed from the side of her mouth. Careful to make sure Catherine couldn't overhear. James didn't agree but took joy out of Matthew's shame all the same, "No, I don't think so. I reckon it's all part of her tactics to get him performing better. She probably heard about what happened in the competition the other day. When push comes to shove, she won't hesitate to back him."

Once everyone had received a book, Catherine began their first lesson. It was from a time before The Controller and the Whiteflyers even existed, "Hundreds of years ago, there was only one world. It was called Persavius. Everyone there was born with the powers of Air, Fire, Water and Earth, albeit some were stronger and more prominent than others. It was very similar to the Earth you know, with similar country lines and borders. The leaders of these lands were rightfully chosen based on their skills with the four powers, and for some time the country lines were respected. But in Persavius, just like Torpor, Arcadius and Tartarus, the people didn't die, and as the population of the world grew, so did the greed.

"Previous leaders no longer accepted when it was time to forfeit their throne to a new and more powerful heir. They grew scared, in constant denial that it was the rightful and only fair way to choose a land's leader. They began to expand their following to gather armies of protectors by crossing country borders and challenging the other leaders to battles, taking their lands and their people as their own. The world was in ruins. Lands were burnt and mountains were moved. Order was completely absent. This continued for 200 years, before structure was once again brought to the world. During that time, nobody was safe. There are far worse things than death in a world where everyone can freely influence the world's natural elements. This is one of the main reasons the Whiteflyer induction process is what it is today. That period proved to the human race that not everyone is capable of handling the responsibility that comes with being able to master the four powers; Air, Fire, Water and Earth."

For the rest of the morning, Catherine made the recruits take turns reading about the time of Persavius in great detail. She occasionally stopped to answer questions and turn on people she didn't think were listening. While James enjoyed learning about the first world, he didn't think the lengthy paragraphs and intricate details were necessary. He would have been more than happy to move on to the next chapter after Catherine's initial overview at the beginning of their lesson. Stevie on the other hand seemed to have a different mindset completely. She surprised James by asking questions and getting involved. She even shushed him at one point when his mind began to wander and he started to chat to her about their training the day before. He didn't know why, but he had never taken her to be the studious type until now.

At the end of the lesson, the recruits brought their history books back to their living quarters for evening reading until their next lesson. James wasn't happy at the thought of being given extra work that would take time away from honing his practical skills. By the end of the week, they would have learnt enough about Air to be able to train alone in the evenings, and he planned to put all of his attention there. Catherine had told them that at the end of the two months they'd have to do a final essay on the history of the worlds, that would be taken into account when they were choosing the ten newest Whiteflyers. She didn't go into detail about how much it was worth but did state that in the past it had been used to decide between recruits with similar power levels.

"I didn't realise that you were so interested in history," James remarked to Stevie on their way out to the training grounds.

"Mm yeah I suppose I am. It was my favourite subject in school. It was the only one I got As in. That's not the only reason I've been showing an interest though. If we want to best the system, we've got to learn as much about it as possible."

James could see the sense in that, but he also didn't think that The Controller would let the Whiteflyers teach them anything that could be damaging to his regime, "Yeah I get where you are coming from but just remember that the class will have selective teachings."

Stevie smiled, "Leave that to me. If you listen closely enough, and ask the right questions, you can find out exactly what you need to know." From the look on Stevie's face James guessed she'd already learnt something valuable, but before he could ask what that was, they'd arrived at the pitch.

"I hope your first class with Catherine Avery was as insightful and interesting as any of the lessons you've received on this practice pitch. Knowing the reasons we are here today is just as important as gaining skill with the powers. Maybe even more important," Vask addressed the recruits who responded with uncoordinated yes' and mumbles before he moved on;

"Today is the day you have probably been most excited for since you were told you were going to discover how to manipulate Air. Today you will begin to learn how to use it to move yourself. Some Whiteflyers like to call it flying, but hovering is the more accurate term." The recruit's energy immediately lifted at the word flying, and a buzz of excitement and whispers flew through the grounds. "Now to begin, I need the current top five recruits to stand forward when you hear your name. Annabelle White, James Moore, Tessa Higgins, Matthew Avery, and Dennis Reilly." He strongly emphasised the word current to remind everyone that they all still had an equal shot at making the final cut.

"Now as you've been told, manipulating Air effectively is largely down to how you distribute the weight of the object. The more irregularly shaped the object, the harder it is to move without one side gravitating towards the ground. With your body, if you distribute more air to one side you will fall over. Your right, left, front, and back should all hold the same amount of air if you want it to keep you up. And in a similar way lifting objects, you will need to push air under your body as it rises off the ground." James was intently listening to everything Vask was saying, determined to be the first in the class to hover. He was well versed in air distribution when he was lifting objects, but he had never moved something as big, heavy, or as weirdly proportioned as himself. Objects that were much longer than they were wide were always difficult to manoeuvre so his height wouldn't come as an advantage in this situation. On the other hand, the closer objects were to his body the easier it was, and you couldn't get closer than moving yourself.

After a few more instructions and the goal to stay off the ground for a full count to 100, the five chosen recruits got to work, each as competitive as the next. To Vask's obvious displeasure, but something he had stated he was expecting, all of their first attempts were rushed and not one of them managed to stop themselves from falling. James went again, this time going as slow as he could, moving the air as necessary as he felt his body tilting. He managed a bit better and stayed up a little longer, but the end result was the same as the first. Before his fifth attempt, James realised that the people on the side-lines were gasping and chatting enthusiastically. A quick glance up told him why. Vask was circling a steadily floating Annabelle, carefully inspecting her form. James quickly put his focus back onto his own powers, but it was too late and the competition was called to a close, Annabelle announced as the winner.

James sauntered back to Stevie frustrated that he didn't pick it up as quickly as he had the flower, but his mood was lifted almost immediately when he saw how Matthew was taking the news. His eagerness to impress, likely fuelled by Catherine's indifferent reaction to him earlier that day, resulted in a more unbearable Matthew than usual. "This is completely unfair. She's a foot shorter than me and much lighter, of course she is going to find it easier at first. Give me someone my own height and build, I will beat them any day." He ranted to Tim louder than he likely meant to, blinded by his own rage.

James jumped to challenge him but Watson, who was standing nearby, removed the need. "Don't be so sure of yourself Matthew. From where I was standing Moore would have beaten you to it with energy to spare. I'd say you're both similar heights and builds would you not?" Too scared to argue back at a Whiteflyer, Matthew didn't respond and instead turned to James, attempting to burn daggers through him with his unmoving stare.

"Everyone find yourself a patch of sand and get to work. We aren't going to divide into groups today. I want 90 people in the air by the end of the day," Vask shouted, diffusing the tension amongst the recruits.

It turned out Watson was right about James, and after a few more attempts he was able to balance steadily in the air. He spent the rest of the day perfecting it and trying to bring himself higher and higher. He'd managed to get nearly two metres off the ground by the time the day was called to an end by the loud bell. The next day, and their last day learning Air for the next few weeks, he was going to practice moving while he hovered. That's when it would get really difficult. Stevie also had a great day and for the first time she was included in the top ten recruits at their end of day ranking. James couldn't help but feel a burst of pride when her name was called out and she smiled the biggest smile he had seen on her face yet. To make the day even better, Matthew was performing dismally. The pressure had gone to his head since his outburst, and after James successfully caught up with Annabelle, his concentration had blown up. Even Tim was doing better than him and had managed to get a few inches off the floor without falling.

7. "WE SHOULD HAVE DONE MORE."

On the last day of Air training, the recruits woke up eager to learn as much as they could before they moved on to working with Fire. They could still spend their evenings in the indoor training room practicing their Air skills but the Whiteflyer trainers wouldn't be on hand to instruct them or teach them any new tricks.

For the second time in two days, as they lined up to leave their dormitory, the drudge that collected them turned right instead of left out into the oval. However, instead of going up the stairs towards Catherine Avery's class, today they were escorted into the domed entrance hall where a few dozen of the Whiteflyers gathered, including Hatt who they hadn't seen since their first day in the headquarters. "It's the weekly announcement. I completely forgot about it. I guess we have to be there," Stevie whispered to James just before the bell went off and the double doors opened. The Whiteflyers walked out first, and the recruits were motioned to follow. James looked out onto the waiting residents and instantly felt ashamed and embarrassed to be standing amongst these people. He remembered how he had felt in that crowd, disgusted at Hatt's condescending and patronising words, yet now he was one of them.

The Torpor residents didn't know the real reason he was up there, and from the looks of disgust on their faces he wasn't sure they'd even understand if he told them.

James didn't listen to Hatt's speech, twice was enough. Instead, he searched the crowd for the people he may have met while he was in Torpor. Tracey and Anne came to mind. He really hoped they weren't watching. He hadn't seen Tracey since first waking up in Torpor and he was unsure of what she'd think watching him stand up on the stage, but he imagined it wouldn't be great. It would seem like a declaration of acceptance to how things were run in the Three Worlds. She was the only person here that he knew of that he'd also known on Earth. His dad's father died before he was born and his mum was still alive. His mum's parents both died in Ireland so even if they were in Torpor they wouldn't be in London. He had a few dead great aunties and uncles that he had met a few times, but he wasn't even sure they would recognise him and he them.

When the speech was over, Hatt had the recruits step forward. They had climbed onto the stage in front of everyone the week before, but their backs would have been to the audience. This was the first time they were being officially introduced to Torpor as official soldiers of The Controller. Vask had previously mentioned that Hatt enjoyed giving sporadic updates to the residents about how they were performing and what they had learnt. It was his way of distilling enthusiasm into the onlookers in the hopes that they would be inspired to sign up the following year. It wasn't until then that James noticed Anne a few rows from the front. She was staring at him and then Stevie intently, with a strong look of confusion on her face. "Anne is down there. Over to the right, around seven rows from the front," James quietly whispered to Stevie from the side of his mouth.

"I see her. We should have explained that we were leaving. She's probably been wondering where we've gone to. This doesn't look right." James peered down the line to get a better idea of what she would be looking at. The other Whiteflyers, all smiled joyfully down at the crowd, proud and happy to be presented to Torpor. A few, including Rowe and Matthew even waved enthusiastically as if they were celebrities at a meet and greet. All James could do was offer Anne a measly yet reassuring smile before avoiding eye contact for the rest of the announcement.

On the way back inside James stopped in his tracks. He could hear a despicable conversation coming from two brutish familiar looking Whiteflyers. They were gaily discussing the Torpor residents. "They're pathetic. Sometimes I wish they'd step out of line more often. That way we could have a bit of fun with them," the fat one declared to the taller of the two.

"Ha! Like their good behaviour has ever stopped us before. It's easy enough to get them riled up if we want them to."

"Yeah but it's just not as fun. I want someone with a bit more fire. Someone that really thinks they've got a shot." James opened his mouth to volunteer, he would have loved nothing more than to punch either of them in the face, but a hand on his arm pressured him to hesitate.

"It's not the time," Stevie grunted under her breath. "They have a say in who becomes a Whiteflyer. I remember them from the first day of training. They'll be our teachers for one of the powers." Biting his tongue and clenching his fist James resisted, instantaneously remembering that that was the reason they looked familiar. Even though she was right, it didn't make him feel any less cowardly, if anything it just heightened his shame after seeing Anne.

For the remainder of the day, Stevie and James made a silent agreement to forego thinking and talking about how they were feeling after such an emotional morning. It was their last day to get the most out of Air before they moved onto Fire the next day, so it was crucial they didn't distract themselves. It resulted in both of them having a productive lesson, learning how to move while they were in the Air, even if it was just for a few seconds. That day, Vask also let everyone in on the secret behind how the Whiteflyers make their voice travel. It was actually easier to do than it looked, involving moving the air as they spoke, but the distance James had seen Catherine, Vask and Hatt make it go was something James aspired to.

At the end of the week's last lesson, Vask had the recruits stand in five lines in front of him as Hatt, Catherine, and the other Whiteflyers from their first day of training came out to meet them. He made a brief speech about the progress they were making as a group and the areas that they needed to practice on over the next few weeks before taking a more individual assessment of each recruit. "While you have made great progress when I look to the group as a whole, there are still weak links that are dragging the other candidates down and taking up our trainer's valuable time. Time that could be spent honing the skills of the people that show true promise. Can the following ten recruits please step to the front, Jane Howard, Rebecca Crossan, Stanley Crochet, Emma Lowe, Richard Taylor, Don Golden, Kate Smith, John Cooper, Naomi Allen and Penelope Price." As the names were called out, the chosen recruits' faces sank. Stepping out, Richie glared back at James and Stevie. The pleading wide look in his eyes aroused a pang of nauseousness to crawl up James' throat. It was obvious to anyone that had been in training that this couldn't be good news. The ten chosen people had been performing consistently worse than the other recruits.

Vask continued, his face impossible to read, "It has been decided that you will all be cut from the training programme, effective immediately. No recruit that hasn't mastered level 4 Air and level 3 Fire has made it to Whiteflyer status and your progress over the last week has confirmed that Air will not be in your grasp by the end of the two months." At that moment, a drudge came out and stopped at the door, Vask gestured to him with an outstretched arm before adding, "Please follow the drudge to your left to begin your next 100 years of service to The Controller and the Three Worlds." Unsurprisingly to James, nobody moved, all of them seemingly stuck to the spot of sand they resided on.

"No this isn't fair. We were told we had two months," Kate whimpered, tears streaming down her face.

"We're not going anywhere. This isn't what we agreed to," Richie continued. Kate's tears prohibited her from arguing further.

"Let me be very clear, I didn't ask you to do anything, I am very much ordering you to. We are positive that none of you will make it past training, so I see no value of delaying the inevitable. Now, do as I say and follow the drudge waiting at the door," Vask said sternly, still keeping his voice level steady.

Once again none of them shifted and as the air grew anxious, Rebecca, a member of Matthew and Tim's posse turned around, "You're our friends, aren't you? Don't let them do this to us. We wouldn't let them take you. We have to stick together." When nobody said anything, scared they'd also be victimised, she turned to

Matthew, "Speak to your great grandmother, explain that we're not affecting your progress."

Matthew turned to look at Catherine who was patiently waiting for his response with narrow eyes before turning back to Rebecca, "It's like Vask said, there's no point in delaying the inevitable."

Before anyone could utter anything further Hatt stepped forward, "I see no reason to entertain this any longer. If anything, this is further proof that none of you are Whiteflyer material. There is absolutely no room for disobedient or cowardly members." With that, Hatt clicked his fingers for dramatic effect and to everyone's, including the other Whiteflyer's surprise, Rebecca went up in flames.

The ear piercing screams that followed were unlike anything that James had ever heard before. Instinctively he ran forward, but with no knowledge of how to control Water to put it out, he didn't know how he could help. Stevie and a few others also ran forward searching for a way to make it stop but the heat made it impossible to get close to her. All they could do was watch as she flayed in the sand desperately trying to put it out before eventually passing out.

The recruits stared at Hatt, shock and horror covering their faces. "Anybody still have any objections to following the drudge waiting at the door?" Hatt asked casually, as if nothing out of the ordinary had just happened. Immediately the nine remaining recruits obeyed, turning and moving inside. Just then, Elizabeth stepped forward, summoning the now extinguished Rebecca to float alongside her as she followed the newest drudges into the building.

As they walked back to their living quarters, the recruits didn't say a word. They were still completely disturbed about what they'd just witnessed. Even Tim looked like he was going to be sick, but James had a feeling that it had more to do with how close he was to becoming a drudge because of his failings over the last week, than it had to do with what had just happened to Rebecca.

"We should have done more," Stevie said, her voice cracking, as she lay onto her mattress.

Sitting on his bed opposite her, James lifted his hands off his head, "I'm replaying it over and over in my head. Trying to figure out how I could have stopped it. I should have gone for Hatt, but would that have even made a difference?"

"No, it just would have set him off on you as well. He is one of, if not the most, powerful Whiteflyers in Torpor, it would take a much bigger distraction than you to get him to lose focus," Stevie replied reassuring herself as well as James.

"Well then what about the fire extinguishers in the Fire section? I could have made a run for them."

Stevie looked at him, pity filling her eyes, "It's not your fault James. None of us thought of it, it happened so fast."

James sighed, he knew she was right, but even still, if he had at least tried his conscience might be clear. Well clearer anyway. "Matthew didn't even flinch. I'd say the rest of his posse don't feel so safe now. We need to make a promise to each other. If and when we become Whiteflyers we need to change how things are run around here. After seeing Anne and now this. I've been thinking more about The Controller and for all we know he doesn't even know what's going on in Torpor. He rarely leaves Arcadius, maybe this isn't how it's supposed to be." Stevie slowly nodded her head in agreement, but her face said something different, she didn't seem to think The Controller would care about how the residents of Torpor were being treated.

Before they went to sleep that night, James and Stevie re-joined the rest of the recruits in the living area. They were anxiously discussing what had unfolded only hours before. "I don't know why she was looking to me to fix it anyway. I've never even met Catherine before coming to Torpor, she's my great grandmother," Matthew reassured the others and himself.

"That's rich. Only a few days ago you were telling everyone how closely knit your family was but now you don't know her? Rebecca was your friend, you could have at least tried to say something," Stevie snarled at him as she took a seat on one of the sofas.

"Nobody was talking to you Miller," Matthew bit back. "Catherine wasn't the one who did it anyway, it was Hatt, and to be quite frank they should have all just followed the drudge when they were asked. If you're useless, you're out. That's the deal."

James could see Stevie getting heated so stepped in before she got herself in trouble. After the bath experience he didn't trust Matthew not to hurt her. "Well if that's the case, Tim over here should start packing his bags. I reckon he just missed getting picked by the skin of his teeth. I for one would swap out Richie for Tim any day."

At the mention of his name Tim snapped his head towards James, "Ooo standing up for your girlfriend are you James? Didn't I hear somcone saying you killed your last one? I'd watch out if I were you

Stevie, you can't die here but as we saw earlier there are worse things on Torpor than death."

As he flashed a toothy grin, James saw red and launched forward, but an awaiting Marcus had anticipated his rage and was blocking his path, "Calm down James. There's been enough drama for one night. Forget about them. They're not worth it." It took everything he had but James let Marcus pull him back into the bedroom.

Stevie didn't follow behind them and James appreciated it. She knew that Liza was the one topic where he wouldn't like her comforting him. "Why do you let them get to you mate?" Marcus asked once James had noticeably calmed down.

"They're the worst kind of people. Somebody has to stand up to them, they will be no better than Hatt in a few years."

Marcus sighed and looked at James confused, "Whether you like him or not, Hatt is going to be your boss if you make it past the next few rounds, which we both know you will. Why did you sign up if you're that against everything?"

James avoided his eyes, Marcus had been one of his favourite recruits, not including Stevie of course, but that didn't mean he trusted him enough to tell him anything, "Let's just say I've got a competitive streak. What about you? You don't seem like those guys, why did you sign up?"

"I was in the army on Earth. Following orders and keeping control is what I do. I don't like all of the Whiteflyers, but that doesn't mean I don't respect them. I learnt pretty quickly once I joined up that sometimes bad stuff has to be done for the greater good. Those that do it, don't necessarily want to." James didn't respond and instead lay back and closed his eyes. He was right to not trust anyone here, they were all as bad as each other and Marcus had just confirmed that. He woke up briefly when the other recruits got into bed but for the most part James fell into a long dark sleep. It had been a long day.

8. "I WAS ANGRY."

While they waited for the drudge to collect them for their first day of Fire, James replayed his conversation with Marcus to Stevie. "Yeah, but I suppose that makes sense if he was in the army before. He's used to believing whatever his 'leader' says is true," Stevie responded, happy that James was talking to her again as if nothing was said about them the night before.

"I guess so, but he just seems so normal, like any of my friends on Earth. I know I said at the beginning that we couldn't trust anyone here, but I was starting to think that he, and maybe even Annabelle, would be on our side if push came to shove with the other Whiteflyers. I was thinking about everything in the bath this morning and if we are serious about changing how things are run in Torpor, we need more than just the two of us. If you look at us from the outside, we are only two inexperienced recruits."

Stevie raised her eyebrow, "Speak for yourself, and if and when the time comes, we won't be two inexperienced recruits. We will be two inexperienced Whiteflyers."

James smiled, but it was all the same. Once he became a Whiteflyer he figured he'd somehow have to try to find some more help. If he couldn't find it in Torpor, he'd have to look further afield and if Tartarus was as bad as he'd been told, some of their Whiteflyers might be more willing to help. He didn't imagine those living lavishly in Arcadius would have much to complain about. "Yesterday put it all into perspective for me, seeing Anne's disappointed face and then after what Hatt did... It's more than just about finding Liza and your mother now. We need to fix things here. I'm not stopping until we rid the worlds of their oppressors."

Stevie nodded in agreement. "I'm with you. I didn't really sleep last night. I was awake trying to picture how different things could be, but right now there are just too many unknowns. But no matter how I look at everything, there is only one next logical step, and that is becoming Whiteflyers and travelling to Arcadius to see The Controller. There's nothing we can do until we find out how to travel between the Three Worlds."

That day in training, the four Whiteflyers that had been training them the previous week had been replaced with four new people. This time all specialising in Fire. There was one friendly-looking woman and three men. James instantly recognised two of them from the conversation he overheard after the weekly announcement the morning before. Vask didn't mention anything about Rebecca or what had happened the day previous, but their missing presence could easily be felt. Whether that was to do with the group shrinking in size or the spectacle of cutting them from the training programme, James was unsure.

"Now that you have all learnt the basics of Air, you will be expected to keep up and develop your skills in the indoor training room. Having the same level of power when we commence Air training again in a few weeks' time will not be acceptable," Vask announced.

Stevie glared at James and he immediately knew what she was thinking, *What if they were next?*

When Vask broke everyone into four groups James was happy to see that neither Matthew nor Tim were put with him. He had just about enough of both of them since their fight about Liza the night before. The further away he was from them the better in his opinion. Tartarus and Arcadius were still too close, but for now he would have to settle on having different trainers. He was also content that their teacher for the day was the light haired woman over the two power hungry morons. "I don't know if you remember me from the first day of your training, but my name is Alice Williams. I've been in Torpor for nearly 300 years now, and a Whiteflyer for 250. As you have probably assumed by now, Fire is my specialty.

"Fire is one of the most dangerous powers out of them all in a lot of ways. If you don't know how to properly work with it, you can easily set yourself and the things around you up in flames. You need to be well versed in extinguishing it if needs be. In order to be able to properly control it, you also need to know how to control Air. That is why the first and most important lesson I am going to teach you will only involve Air. Let me demonstrate." The recruits watched as Alice made a show of swaying her clothes side to side with the air surrounding her. She then summoned enough fire to cover her hands and slowly moved it so it was also covering the arm of her robe. "Don't be scared. Take a closer look." As he walked forward, James realised what Alice was bringing their attention to. Like he had seen with Vask that day in Stevie's old house, there was a thin layer of air between her robes and the fire.

"The air, it stops the material from burning," Tessa proclaimed loudly.

Alice nodded, looking around to make sure everyone clearly understood, "Very good. While the Fire you summon yourself won't burn your body, it will set your clothes on fire. So, unless you're looking to undress very quickly, I would suggest putting an air pocket in its way. This can also be handy if you need to protect anything else around you from the fire. More of that will come later, but for now, can I have a volunteer?"

A few people looked to James expecting him to nominate himself like he had done the week before, but truth be told he wasn't in the mood to do anything that a Whiteflyer asked him to do just yet. Even though Alice wasn't personally responsible for anything that had happened the day before, he swiftly decided to stick this one out. Surprisingly however, Stevie didn't have the same urge to feel in control and stepped forward. She never was one for holding grudges or shifting the blame. "I'd like to give it a go. I'm Stevie, Stevie Miller."

"Okay Stevie. Close your eyes and concentrate on my instructions." Stevie did as she asked, clearing her mind and focusing completely on what Alice was asking of her. She knew some of the people in the group underestimated her, most notably Rowe, and she aimed to prove them wrong. "The flames come from your body heat, it's a thermal energy inside of you. The hotter you are, the more easily you will be able to light a fire. I need you to find that energy and concentrate on it. Match it to your power source, the same tingle you use for Air and will also use for Water and Earth and bring it out through your skin. For now, just focus on it leaving through your hand. Try not to let it exit your body anywhere near your robes."

At that last sentence, a few of the people in the group stood back, but James didn't move. Carefully watching Stevie put all of her effort into lighting the small flame. Silently urging her on. Within ten minutes a small ball of flame appeared and then disappeared just as fast in the palm of her hand. Stevie stayed silent and focused, even as the class "Ooed and awed", and once again the ball of flame materialised. This time staying put, flickering gently in the light wind. Stevie opened her eyes and stared down at her hand in shock. "I did it. I actually did it," she yelled to James excitedly, not caring who heard her. Seeing the joy on her face stirred something not unlike butterflies inside James' stomach but a sudden flash of Liza appearing in his head pushed them to the side. He turned his head away from the crowd, as he felt himself growing redder, confused and irritated by his reaction.

For the remainder of the day the recruits learnt how to conjure Fire. Because they were already used to working with their power source it was a lot easier for the majority of them to grasp the initial first step than it had been with Air and by the end of the day some of them, including James and Stevie, were even learning how to expand the fire over their hand.

For the most part, James had blocked out the other groups of recruits, so he was unsure of how anyone else had been getting on until the end of day rankings. During Air training the same names had kept popping up again and again at the front of the leader board every evening, but both fortunately and unfortunately for James there were some new additions added to the list now that they'd moved onto Fire. James, Matthew, Tessa, and Annabelle all still resided near the top, but some unlikely additions included Stevie, Rufus and even Tim.

"Looks like Tim stands a chance after all," Stevie sighed as they finished off their first solo Air practice in the indoor training room. James didn't respond and instead shrugged his shoulders and floated back to the ground, attempting to play off how irked he was as nonchalance. Stevie didn't push it, turning the conversation back into a replay of how their first Fire lesson had gone.

For the rest of the week, the recruits spent their days honing and growing their Fire skills. While Stevie wasn't particularly great at learning how to manipulate Air, she was picking up the knack of Fire a lot quicker. James was just as good as he had been the week before and was almost always ranked at the top of his group. By now they knew how to cover their bodies, robes and all, in flames. They had even learnt the basics of how to move the fire away from their bodies. As it involved using both air and fire simultaneously, it was proving to be difficult, but Vask assured them that it was something they would learn to master in the second phase of their lessons.

Matthew had also been performing quite well and even Tim's performance from the first day didn't waver for the rest of the week. As James expected, they had both gravitated towards the two blonde bullish trainers that he now knew as Charlie and Alton. James and Stevie had to endure a whole day of training listening to Tim suck up to Charlie and bad mouth James when they were all grouped together.

However, even though there had been some advancements in the rankings, not all of the recruits were showing as much skill in Fire and after the first day of training it was evident to see why it was a level three power while Air was a level four. Especially considering a lot of the safety aspects of it required having some of the knowledge they had learnt during their first week. The fire extinguishers and sprinklers had definitely come in handy.

To Stevie's amusement, Rowe was one of the recruits that was finding it hard to grasp the basics of it and at one point she even charred the end half of her hair off after falling into Lily's flames. The recruits were kept awake by wailing sounds emerging from her bunk for half of the night after that, but it was well worth it to some of them to know that Rowe was getting kicked off her high horse.

Fire was proving to be a really enjoyable power to work with and overall, James was having a much better week than he had had previously. Ignoring Matthew and Tim was proving to be the more mature option that he had considered over the nights and he hadn't gotten into an argument with anyone since the night Tim told him he had killed Liza.

James even found the history class interesting where they had learnt about The Controller's early life. "Nearly seven hundred years ago, The Controller was born in London's equivalent of Persavius," Catherine had explained. "He was quickly proven to wield a power far stronger than anyone born before him. His ability to influence the four elements was like nothing that was ever seen before. The most powerful ruler at that time was a wicked manipulative woman who controlled all of Europe's lands. She was heading to America to attempt to overthrow a ruler there, when she heard of a child who was showing promise far more than she ever had. She paused her plans and attempted to imprison The Controller before he had a chance to grow up. She didn't want to conquer America only to come back and find a boy, much younger and less experienced than she was, displacing all the years of work she'd put into establishing Europe as her own.

"However, even at a young age The Controller easily defeated her. With no real allegiance, and running on fear alone, the woman's armies bowed down to their rightful leader. After years of torment, balance was starting to be restored in Persavius. However, the land's borders had undergone too much turmoil to be reinstalled. The Controller, knowing nobody else was trusted to selflessly govern the whole of Persavius, took it upon himself to rebuild the world." While Catherine's spin on the events implied that The Controller had no choice but to take power over the lands the woman had ruled, James found it extremely difficult to believe that his rule was completely selfless. Nonetheless, even though he never enjoyed sit down classes at school, he had to admit that he was eager to learn more about The Controller and found he was looking forward to Catherine's class every week. Now that he and Stevie were aiming to fix the balance of power on Torpor, and maybe even Arcadius and Tartarus, anything they learnt was not only entertaining, but it may just turn out to be vital to their cause.

During the second half of their last day of Fire training, the recruits stood up one by one and pushed their fire abilities to the limit in front of Vask, the other trainers, and Hatt and Catherine who had just joined them to witness the spectacles. The evening before the recruits were up late anxiously discussing how many people they thought were going to get cut. If what Hatt said was true the week before, this would be the last time they would eliminate people before the final week. Not all of the Whiteflyers mastered Water and Earth, so while it was a benefit it wasn't a necessity if they wanted to be one of the final ten, so it wasn't likely they'd be making any more early eliminations after Fire.

When Stevie's turn came around, James could hear Rowe and Tessa sniggering off to the side, attempting to throw her off her game. He glared at Rowe, the likely leader, until she looked over and mimed, "Nice hair." To save from crying, she immediately stopped laughing and roughly elbowed Tessa to follow her lead. Stevie's performance got a smile and a nod from Alice, which instantly calmed James' mood just in time for his turn to come around. She was safe for now.

As he sat and watched the recruits, James quickly tried to think up something to do. He quite liked how Annabelle made the fire flow around her body, almost as if they were waves in the sea. Harper also put on a surprisingly good performance and spelt out Torpor on the ground with fire. He couldn't steal any of those ideas though. If he wanted to do well, he would need to come up with something original.

"Moore you're up next," Vask announced, as Rowe who showcased an average level of skill sat down, her face sour and unsatisfied. James stood up and decided instantly that he was going to aim for one of the target boards a couple of metres away to his right. The recruits hadn't practiced using the boards yet, they had been told they'd have plenty of time to use them once they'd learnt the basics and moved on to the more advanced level of making fire travel away from their body.

As James turned towards them, Alton piped up, "Ooh we have a ballsy one."

With Matthew then adding, "Let's hope it's not a car crash." James whipped his head around in time to see Matthew wink. He was trying to wind him up, knowing it worked perfectly well when Tim had brought up the accident before.

"Breathe. Don't listen to him," he whispered to himself as he felt his temper rising.

"At least this time he's the only one who will suffer if it is," Rowe replied loudly to a laughing Matthew. James couldn't help himself, he could feel a surge of anger building up inside of him and without fully registering what he was doing he aimed everything he had at the target board in front of him and then at the one beside it and then again at the one beside that. Before he fully registered what had happened, all ten target boards were set alight. James realised he was holding his breath and took a deep gulp of fresh air that instantly relaxed him. The oval had gone eerily quiet and he felt embarrassed knowing how obvious he had made it that Matthew and Rowe had got to him.

Slowly he peered his head around, but the faces staring back at him weren't smiling or smug, they were in shock. "How did you do that?" Hatt demanded, addressing him personally for the first time. As he did, Vask blew a strong gust of wind at the targets, simultaneously putting the fires out.

"Em I don't know, it just happened," Matthew responded, lowering his voice and adding, "I was angry." The Whiteflyers, wide eyed, turned in to huddle together. The silence was replaced by hurried murmurs before Vask, eyeing James with confusion mixed with a touch of pride, asked him to take a seat and called the next person up to demonstrate what they'd learnt.

"You never told me you could do that!" Stevie uttered from the side of her mouth, as they watched the last recruits try and even mildly impress the Whiteflyers after James' display.

"Well, I didn't know I could do it, did I? I just got so heated and I don't know, I guess that's what happens when we are angry and have powers."

Stevie shook her head from side to side, "I don't know James, even the Whiteflyers looked slightly impressed and super surprised. You're only supposed to know the basics by now. We haven't even gone onto target practice yet. You should have seen Matthew's face, he thought he was definitely going to be ranked first after moving the flames a few inches away from his hands."

To nobody's surprise, James was ranked first in the class. He even got a wink from Hatt, who he had never seen show anyone any sign of approval, Whiteflyer or recruit. While he was elated that he was picking everything up so fast, his attempt to hide his grin was made easy when the ten recruits that were being kicked out were called out.

This time they made no fuss and sullenly left the grounds without argument. Stevie and James hadn't really talked to many of the chosen ones much, but all the same, it was a harsh reminder of how quickly everything could be taken away. All of their hopes and plans could be quashed just as quickly as they were conceived if they were not picked as Whiteflyers.

9. "YOU CAN MANIPULATE WATER."

The next day at training, Vask made a short speech about how there would be no more people cut from the recruits until after their final challenge. James couldn't help but feel relieved for Stevie. While she was by no means one of the worst in the class, she had her nervous moments, and an off day could prove detrimental if they were performing for Vask, Hatt and Catherine. After introducing their newest trainers, who would be teaching them how to control Water, Vask gave them their first brief idea of what they might expect from the final competition, "Every week, and sometimes two or three times a week, we have been holding challenges to try to test your limits and get a better idea of who has what it takes to become a Whiteflyer. For your final test, while there will be an allocated time for freestyling, you will also be marked on your ability to complete a course designed specially to discover how your Air, Fire, Water, and Earth skills have progressed. This will determine whether or not you have mastered each level and which powers you will be allowed to keep if you are chosen to become a Whiteflyer. While I only expect the very best of you to master Water, I hold high hopes that you will all surprise me. Only between four and six people show a high enough level of skill every year to keep it. I expect this group to be on the higher end. We won't be giving anyone an insight into what the desired level for Water is until after you have demonstrated your powers at the final competition, so there is no room to get complacent."

The Water grounds were the most interesting yet, taken up by nearly all water with walkways running up and down and from side to side for the recruits and trainers to get around. Mixing things up, Vask split up some of the friendship groups and assigned Stevie and James to separate groups. James's trainer was an older bodied stern man who could have been an army commander or even a school principal in a previous life. He went by the name of Black, "Unlike Air and Fire, Water cannot be conjured in every environment. You need to be in its presence in order to manipulate it, it can't appear from nothing. Also, unlike Air and Fire, it is a power that requires movement, as it follows the path you give it. If everyone spreads out onto the walkways, I will demonstrate."

When they did as they were told, Black carefully lifted his arm from his side, and reached out in front of him. The water directly opposite his hand followed suit, moving up and down in tune with his outstretched hand. He then lifted his left arm to the side and another small bubble of water jumped out of the pool, once again following his movements. "Cool!" Tim exclaimed, moving his arm to try and copy Black.

"Nice try recruit but it's not as easy as that," Black snorted. Embarrassed, Tim yawned and reached his arm into the air, unsuccessfully trying to fool everyone into thinking that he had been merely stretching and that Black wasn't referring to him.

"Everyone! Concentrate on a spot of water in front of you and locate your power source, bringing it into your right hand. Your body is full of water, it runs through every cell of your body. You need to concentrate all of your energy on getting the tingle to stick to that water. Force them to become one. Once they do, the water you are directing your physical and mental attention at will link to it, driving the water where you direct it to go." James tried to do as he was asked but he didn't know how he was supposed to locate his body's water in the first place. While he had learnt his body was made up of water in school, it wasn't as if he could feel, hear or see it. Looking around, it seemed everyone was pretty much in the same boat, with a few people looking like they were close to giving themselves a hernia, desperately trying to make the water move.

"Sorry Mr Black, but this doesn't seem to be working. Can we have another hint on how to get it started?" Annabelle asked, yawning mid-sentence.

Black immediately turned his attention to her, scrunching up his nose as a red flush grew up his pale face. "Firstly, I introduced myself as Black, not Mr Black, you are not in school. Secondly, weren't you listening to Vask? Do I need to get him over here to repeat it for you again? Fewer than 10% of you will master Water, that is only half of those who will get Whiteflyer status. This is not a game, there are no hints or tricks that will speed up the process," Black asserted, balls of spit flying from his mouth. Too frightened to reply, Annabelle nodded enthusiastically and got straight back to work. Nobody dared to question his methods for the rest of the day but even if they were at fault, none of the recruits in any of the other groups managed to make the water move either.

That evening, James and Stevie spent most of their time practicing their Air and Fire powers. Irritatingly, most of the others either practiced alongside them or stood on the side lines and watched. Matthew, Tim, Rowe and six or seven others were the only ones who trained on the opposite side of the room. Since his display with Fire the day before, the recruits were flocking to James, attempting to learn something from him and pestering him to tell them how he did it. However, truth be told, while James was pretty good at Fire, he wasn't entirely sure how he had blown up all of those targets, and he definitely wouldn't be able to explain to anyone how to do it.

"We are friends, aren't we?" Marcus asked James, out of earshot of anyone but Stevie and Annabelle. "Yes, we are, but that doesn't mean I can tell you how I did it," James snapped before Marcus could ask the obvious question. "Never said that you can, but if you could or if you find out how, you'd tell us wouldn't you? I mean, I know I would tell you. We four, getting Whiteflyer status over Matthew and his followers, that's the game plan."

Extinguishing the ball of flame floating out in front of him James rolled his eyes, he couldn't concentrate with everyone pulling at him for advice. "Yeah sure Marcus. I'm finished here. I'm going to take a bath." As some of them went to follow he quickly added, "By myself".

Relaxing alone in the hot water, James began to fall into memories from when he was younger with his sister Jen. He laughed to himself remembering how they used to tease each other. She once baited him into climbing into a suitcase, by insisting that he couldn't fit. She wheeled him to the end of the road once it was zipped up and didn't come back for what felt like hours. In reality it was probably only twenty minutes but the fear of thinking he would never escape turned every minute into half an hour. After that, he got her back by telling her that her birthday present was hidden behind the couch, when the only thing back there was a mouse trap his dad had laid out to capture the little creature that had made his home in their old plumbing pipes. James got seriously scolded after that one, and Jen's fingers still held the scars. Coming back to reality, James decided to practice his Water skills while he was soaking alone. This was the calmest he had felt in a while and he wanted to take advantage of the rare opportunity of getting the bathroom all to himself. Without feeling the pressure of an audience, he idly replayed Black's instructions to himself, following along.

Four, five, and then six attempts passed, and James still didn't manage to make anything happen. He closed his eyes and imagined the bath water going through his body. He pictured it coursing through his veins and flowing through his cells, and all of a sudden something felt different. His hand felt numb but at the same time completely alive, if that was even possible. Instinctively, he concentrated on a patch of water in front of him and reached his hand in the same direction. Before it even happened, he knew it would work. Lifting his arm up, a small puddle of water followed. Testing the limits, he drew circular motions in the air and watched in a trance like state as the water followed. Again and again, he made small bubbles of water react to his commands, shooting them as high into the air as he could before releasing it to drop and moving on to the next one, only stopping when he realised the door was open.

"James... You can manipulate Water. But how? Earlier..." but before Stevie finished, James answered, "I've no idea, but it's cool right? I think it's my favourite power so far." To James' surprise Stevie didn't look happy, if anything she seemed worried, but whatever she was going to say next was cut short with the sounds of the other recruits coming down the hall. They were going to want to shower, and more attention was the last thing James needed. Before even opening his mouth to relay this to Stevie, she responded, "I know. Later."

When everyone had gone to sleep that night James finally got his opportunity to ask Stevie what she was about to say. Out of everyone here, he thought she would be the one to be truly happy for him that he was mastering all of the power levels so quickly. "Oh, I've been going over it and it probably doesn't matter. I am just overthinking everything. It's just a lot to take in is all. You can't deny it's a bit mental to think that just a few weeks ago we didn't even know each other or that these powers even existed."

James couldn't agree more, he was starting to feel like he'd known Stevie his whole life, "I know, it's crazy. But you shouldn't feel weird about me picking up the powers before you do. You did so well in Fire and you've gotten so much better at Air since we've been practicing indoors. You are a shoe in. We are in this together." Stevie smiled at that and opened her mouth to reply but her words fell short when James added, "Don't worry. I'll find Liza and you will find your mum."

Her face dropped a little and she pulled her duvet closer, "It has nothing to do with me James. I would never want you not to do well. Anyway, it doesn't matter, as I said I was just caught by surprise. It's late. Let's just go to sleep." James was a little taken aback by Stevie's sudden change in tone of voice, she was coming across a lot more bluntly than he was used to. But at the same time, she was right, it was late and she was probably just tired.

By the next morning, Stevie was back to her normal upbeat talkative self and showed no more doubt about James' newfound powers. She eagerly discussed her anticipation for the look on Matthew and Tim's faces when they saw how he had progressed overnight. The two of them even stood next to them purposely so that when they were being separated into groups they would likely be put together. James wasn't entirely fussed either way but because it made Stevie happy, he went along with it. Their reaction was just as they had anticipated, and Matthew even pushed Rufus into one of the water pools when he asked him if he thought he was close to getting it. Vask didn't say anything when James' ability was brought to his attention but his face split into an uncustomary grin and he spent some time making notes in the journal he was documenting everyone's progress in. Black was even less impressed and made no sign that it was any more than was expected of everyone.

As the days went on, some of the other recruits began to make better progress with Water. A quarter of them, including Stevie with James' help, had managed to move a ball of it once or twice, and less than a handful had managed every time. Unfortunately, Matthew was in the latter group.

While the recruits had started to admire James after his display with Fire, as time progressed their feelings were beginning to turn into envy and hatred. Even Marcus seemed to be getting a little fed up with James insisting that he wasn't really sure how he was doing it and that it couldn't really be taught. While this was true, Stevie's progress made it seem like he was lying. While he was helping her, it was in more of a moral support sense. That and his encouragement of getting her to keep practicing. By the time Catherine's third class came around she was ranking in the top fifteen of the class.

"Today's lesson is going to cover what happened once The Controller took power," Catherine announced from over her history book at the top of the room. "It wasn't nearly as peaceful as it is today."

James looked over at Stevie, predicting that she would have something to say about Catherine's choice of words. On queue, she lifted her book up enough to just cover her mouth and mouthed, "Peace, prison, same thing I guess."

"As I was saying in our previous lessons, by this time the people of Persavius were beginning to grow restless. Their leaders weren't content with giving up their lands to more powerful rulers and the people were sick of the disruption the fighting was causing to their everyday lives. The worst amongst us began to revolt. Forests were burnt to the ground, and islands were sunk to disappearance. Persavius was in ruins. As the population grew, the problem only worsened, and the world began to overcrowd. When people can reproduce forever, the rate of growth in the population is far quicker than you can begin to imagine.

"To combat this, The Controller did the unthinkable. Being as powerful as he was, he was able to create three new worlds as a reflection of Persavius, using the four powers Air, Fire, Water and Earth. You now know these worlds as Torpor, Arcadius, and Tartarus. It was power unlike anything that was ever seen before, your entire existence can be traced back to that moment. Without it we would undoubtedly have imploded. Because we cannot age in the Three Worlds, unborn children cannot grow. So Persavius, now known as Earth, began one of its most important roles, as a temporary holding ground for people to mature and bring new life into existence. The notion of being able to have children forever was finally stopped." Catherine stopped talking for a moment to let her lesson sink into the dumbstruck faces in front of her. James couldn't believe what he was hearing. The Controller was powerful enough to create three entire new worlds. The possibility of it was astounding. While he always believed that The Controller had powers the rest of them could only dream of, creating three entire new worlds was way past anything he had contemplated.

While James was lost in thought, Stevie saw that this was her chance to get some answers. She shot her hand into the air, hungry to know more, "So when did he decide to separate the people based on their behaviour on Earth? Did everyone still have powers at this point? How did their powers get taken away and why does The Controller still have his?"

Catherine narrowed her eyes before speaking again, but instead of answering Stevie's questions directly, she addressed the class as a whole, "That is enough for everyone to digest for today without having more information added to the mix. Please spend the rest of the morning reading over chapters 4 and 5 and try to get a deeper understanding of what I have just told you. Any questions on what we are going over today, and not in future lessons, please raise your hand."

It was not surprising to anyone who knew her, but still quite shocking that Stevie wasn't satisfied with Catherine's answer, "So are you going to answer my questions next week if I ask them then?"

Catherine clenched her jaw and stared directly into Stevie's eyes, "Don't you dare take that tone with me. I am here to teach you what you need to know, not what you want to. Trust me when I say I won't forget to explain anything that you're permitted to learn."

Once more Stevie wasn't content with the answer to her question. Frustrated, she stood up and raised her voice an octave higher, "You're our teacher, how are we supposed to learn anything if..." but James never heard the end of Stevie's sentence. She had paralysed in mid speech. Her mouth hung open, and her body tightened, only her manically moving eyes showed signs of life.

"What did you do to her?" James pleaded with Catherine, forgetting himself and standing up to be at her and Stevie's level.

"When you have been around as long as I have James, you have time to think of thousands of unique ways to manipulate your powers to get what you want," Catherine answered flippantly, before casually turning to look out the window as if she hadn't just frozen the air surrounding one of her students in place. James desperately tried to move that air, but he was no match for Catherine's powers. "There's no need for that James," Catherine responded to the pressure on the air she was no doubt feeling. "But one more step out of line Stevie Miller, and you will be out of these headquarters before you even have a chance to say goodbye to Mr Moore here." At her last word, Stevie finally moved again, and the panic that was only visible in her eyes before flooded her face.

"Yes Catherine," she responded, before swiftly sitting down and sticking her head into her book.

"What the Tartarus was that?" James angrily demanded of Stevie on their way out onto the training grounds. "You need to play it coy with Catherine, she's one of the three most powerful Whiteflyers in Torpor. Are you trying to get us both kicked out? Stop asking her questions you know she won't like."

Stevie was jotting down information in her book when she looked up, "I don't think it was my questions she didn't like, but more the phrasing of them. I was too confrontational, as if The Controller was to blame. I need to be more careful of that in the future if we want to find answers."

James snorted and added, "Yeah and if you want her to pick you to become a Whiteflyer. She does get a say after all and her say carries a lot of weight."

As the Water week came to a close, only four of the recruits were proficient enough to meet Vask's standards - James, Matthew, Tessa and Rufus. The Whiteflyer trainers didn't hide their disapproval with the group after the closing challenge, with Hatt even threatening to cut more people before the end of the two months if they didn't start improving. Catherine was the only one who didn't comment, which James guessed had a lot to do with Matthew's progress. She seemed like the snooty type who cared more about upholding her family's name over anything else.

Back in their headquarters, the recruits took Hatt's threat as seriously as he meant it and trained harder than before. As a group they had improved a lot since their first week of training, even though the indoor grounds weren't big enough to reach their full potential, and everyday someone amongst them hit their next goal. That night it was Tim, who was finally able to fly. "That was literally the only thing that made me positive he wasn't going to become a Whiteflyer. He was much better at Fire than I expected, so not mastering Air was all that we had against him," Stevie moaned as she juggled with two balls of fire.

"He's not going anywhere after this but to the drudge's quarters. Everyone has improved at both Air and Fire, he's definitely not in the top ten overall," James replied, trying hard to appear confident about what he was saying.

"I am not in the top ten yet either though. I know I always say I'll be picked, but after today's challenge, I've started to doubt myself for the first time."

James grew embarrassed. He was only trying to make her feel better about Tim by insinuating that the current top ten would be the chosen ones. The last thing he wanted was for her to lose hope. "Don't be ridiculous, you're nothing like him. Nobody did well today, Water is harder to grasp than the rest of them, you'll pick it up. Just think about how much you've improved with Air since we started."

A faint smile appeared on her lips and she raised her eyebrow, "Well, not everybody did badly today."

"Oh, shut up. You know what I meant," James said, jumping a meter into the air before he had the chance to grow even redder.

10. "I DIDN'T MEAN TO DIE."

On their first day of Earth training, the recruits lined up in front of Vask in the oval. This morning, no other Whiteflyers stood with him, "As you all know, only eight people that have trained on these grounds have gone on to master Earth. Your trainers for the next week will be some of the most important people in Torpor, and in some cases, in all of the Three Worlds. You will treat them with the utmost of respect, and you WILL NOT embarrass me or yourselves by showing incompetence. Your performances with Water yesterday were disappointing and frankly on the lower side of average. This should not, and will not, be repeated at the end of this week."

James was expecting this today and silently wished Vask would just hurry up and get it over with. He was yearning to begin, and he really didn't see what good fussing over the previous week would do to anyone's confidence. Earth was the power he had been most excited about, the one that very few could grasp. Vask continued on his rampage about the day before for some time, even singling some people out for their less than satisfactory skills, before finally moving on to the present, "In order to accomplish level four, you need to know how to manipulate all twenty three of the materials laid out in front of you, as well as the last one that compiles all of them into one. They are made up of three rock types, sixteen minerals, and three soils. You cannot move onto the next one until I, or the other trainers, are satisfied that you are proficient in the one you are currently assigned to."

Just then the headquarters' doors opened and out walked three of the people that had been hanging on the walls of the recruits indoor training room for the last three weeks. All of the portraits held a small plaque, so James was familiar with them before they even introduced themselves. The first man was Brian Johnson, he had died in 1736 at the age of 37. His long hair and wiry beard were in sharp contrast to the pristine white outfit that marked him as a Whiteflyer. Following behind him was Matilda Brine. She was the most recent person to master all four powers, dying in 1943. Her body stopped ageing at the age of 52, but seeing her in person, James found it hard to believe she was even near that. Her wrinkle free skin, long blonde hair and slender physique gave off the impression that she was in her mid-30s. If she died recently, his mind would have immediately jumped to botox. The last person, and the Whiteflyer Stevie and James were most excited to meet, was Joseph Sage. Dying in 1810, at the mere age of 13, made Joseph not only the youngest Torpor Whiteflyer to master the four powers, but the youngest Whiteflyer in the whole of Torpor's United Kingdom. There weren't many kids in general in Torpor because the majority of them lived too short a life to end up anywhere but Arcadius, but even the ones that were there rarely went on to sign up to become Whiteflyers. He was somewhat of a legend in the headquarters' halls.

Used to having four trainers, the recruits eagerly waited for the fourth person that would be teaching them the skills of Earth to reveal themselves. James was half expecting Hatt to come out of the door or for Catherine to lay down her history teaching hat. Instead however, Vask stepped forward announcing himself as the last trainer. He usually took an overseeing role, but due to the lack of Earth trainers available, he was set to be more hands-on for their last week of basic power training.

In contrast to most days, the recruits weren't split up into four groups. They were instead broken out into groups of twos, with the odd group of three, each assigned a different material. James was paired with Tessa and set to work with some sort of stone. To Stevie's horror, she was paired with Rowe, working with a soil. "In order to manipulate Earth, you need to be grounded somehow. Whether that is standing directly in the soil you wish to reshape or touching one finger off a 100ft building that connects to the stone you want to move. The soles of your shoes are made from a mix of all the materials to make connecting that much easier. The more closely you are connected to it, the easier it will be, but as you have learnt in Catherine Avery's class this week, nothing is impossible," Vask explained, to his alert audience.

Excited whispers began to form at the thought of creating a whole new world, but they were briskly cut off as Vask continued. "Working with earth is not unlike working with water in a lot of ways. It takes a lot of intuition and guess work. While you don't need to move your hands to move and shape Earth, you may find it will focus you. Each of the twenty-three earth materials need to be dealt with differently. The only commonality between them all is that you will need to stretch your power source out through your physical connection with Torpor. The strength of your connection with the material you are looking to manoeuvre is what matters most. If you can form the strongest possible connection, your creativity is your only limit." Looking at the excited faces he added, "However, only The Controller has managed to push his powers to such a limit, so don't get ahead of yourselves."

Unsurprisingly, at the end of their first day, none of the recruits had managed to make a connection with their designated material, but it was a fun day nonetheless. The trainers took a different approach than Black and the other Water instructors and put on more than a few demonstrations. When Vask's head was turned Joseph even created a statue out of limestone in his exact likeness. On top of that, Stevie only managed to get in one brief fight with Rowe over who was taking the longest turns. That quickly ended when Matilda slowly began to sink their bodies into the soil until they sorted it out. They stopped talking when she got to their waists, but James wouldn't have put it past her to have buried them alive. She had a 'just dare me' look in her eyes during it that convinced him she was enjoying it.

Over the next day or two, a couple of the recruits began to adapt their skills for Earth. To James' annoyance, Matthew had progressed onto his fourth material while James was still on his third. Because nobody else, bar Annabelle who was on her second material, had progressed from the first material that they were assigned, James felt like he couldn't vent his frustrations properly to Stevie without her getting sarcastic. He had performed so well on the last three levels that he had subconsciously assumed that the next picture hanging on the wall of the living quarters would be of him. He refused to let Matthew stay ahead of him for much longer, but the more it played on his mind, the worse his concentration got.

On their fourth morning of training that week, James and Stevie sat in the lounge waiting for the drudge to come and collect them. "I mean, I would obviously prefer if you advanced to more materials than Matthew does, but I don't really expect any of us to master Earth, not to the level where you get to keep it anyway. You've seen how few do. The chances really aren't in anyone's favour, so I'm not worried that Matthew will, and you won't. I don't think either of you will," Stevie explained to a moody James. James grunted, this was the exact response he was expecting, but it still didn't make it any less irritating. He would pass Earth; he needed all four powers. Just when he opened his mouth to give a flippant response, the door to the quarters opened and his perspective on everything took a U turn. In walked Richie, head to toe in the black drudge's robes.

Stevie jumped up and ran over. James knew she was hopeful he'd been allowed to come back, but he had realised the real reason he was there almost immediately. "I'm not back Stevie. Don't make this any more embarrassing than it needs to be and just line up so I can escort you outside," Richie pleaded, refusing to make eye contact with any of them.

"What do you mean escort us outside? Surely, they didn't assign you to bring us out to the training grounds. That is just cruel. Are they trying to rub salt in your wounds?" Richie didn't respond, dropping his head and leading the way as a line formed behind him. James could sense a mixture of pride, relief and worry flood the room. Everyone was happy that it wasn't them, but at the same time, they were worried that it might be, one day soon. On the other hand, James didn't feel any of those feelings, all he felt was disgust.

He'd been acting like a spoilt child with an inflated ego. He realised he hadn't really thought about Richie and the others since they'd left, not properly anyway. He was too concentrated on being the best. Why did it even really matter if he beat Matthew? He was all but guaranteed a Whiteflyer position by now, but all he could think about was being even better. The rest of them, including Stevie, were possibly all awaiting a different fate. He needed to take a step back and remember the real reason he was there, whatever the others thought, it had nothing to do with making Whiteflyer history. He recalled Stevie's face when she saw him in the bath throwing the water bubbles into the air and he had a sudden realisation of why. She thought so too. She could see him turning into the person he promised himself he wouldn't be. He was becoming like Matthew and it had to stop there.

After training, James watched as Stevie practiced her Water skills in the bathtub. Keeping his promise to himself, James didn't train with her. The powers didn't matter, it was only becoming a Whiteflyer that did, and Richie had made him realise that. Nobody had got any more information out of their fallen recruit that morning, so it was impossible to know what the drudges went through, but the vacant expression on Richie's face painted an all too vivid picture. It certainly wasn't a holiday that they were sentenced to.

"James, I know what you're thinking, and I know why you haven't been practicing tonight. You weren't even trying today in training and you didn't even flinch when Matthew was moved again." Riddled with guilt, James didn't reply. He was embarrassed enough by how he was acting over the last few days. He didn't want to talk about it any further. "I know you feel guilty about Richie. I do too, but that doesn't mean now is the time to relax. If anything, we need to fight even harder."

"Relax, what do you mean relax?" James spat, angry at Stevie's choice of words. "None of it matters. I'll practice enough to make the top ten, but I don't want these powers going to my head. I realise I've been getting too cocky and arrogant lately. I know that was what you were about to say when you saw me moving the water for the first time last week. It won't happen again."

James prepared himself for Stevie's agreement but shockingly she began to laugh, "James, you melon head. I don't think you've been anything but your protective and slightly competitive self and if anything, this just proves it." When James didn't seem to believe her, she continued, "I was worried when I saw you picking up Water so fast. It was just after the Fire challenge. It seems silly really thinking back, but honestly, I thought you were getting too good. After our history lesson about the old leaders taking down any potential threats, I got worried that you were standing out too much."

James felt a wave of relief wash over him, she didn't hate him, she was worried about him, "Well you should have just told me. I know I am definitely not some prodigy recruit. Yesterday though, you said you don't expect anyone to master Earth. What made you change your mind about me?"

Stevie laughed again, "Well I figured Matthew's not going to easily beat the next all-powerful leader. Let's just say, you definitely still need to practice." James splashed her with water as he waded through to get closer to her. She tried to duck away but he caught her in headlock, brushing the top of her head gently with his knuckles until she submitted, "James is the all-powerful King of the world. I take it back, I take it back."

For the remainder of the week, James went back to giving Earth his all and training as hard as ever after practice in Air, Fire and Water. Stevie had encouraged him to do his best. She explained what he knew himself anyway but was too preoccupied to think about. Even though he didn't need to be the best in the class, he did need to be as good as he could possibly be if they stood a chance of standing up to the other Whiteflyers, and maybe even The Controller, when the time called for it. Because he had lost all notions that he needed to be better than Matthew, he was, naturally. By the end of the week he was on his tenth material with Matthew on his seventh. The other recruits could only look on in envy, with the better of them only having completed three or four materials and the majority still stuck on the first or second one.

For the week's closing challenge, James created a sphere model resembling Persavius, which was not unlike Earth, adding soil, minerals, rock and even water where it was necessary. He copied it from an old image he found in his history book and even Catherine's face looked impressed. It was obvious that she didn't think he would do as well as Matthew had, but James' unexpected addition of Water put him over the edge. By now, Stevie had only managed to manipulate the soil she began on, so really there wasn't much she could do with it. Thankfully, however, it was better than those who were unable to do anything. James had to look the other way as they stood on their material and anxiously willed it to do something.

"A very pathetic attempt," Vask announced, unimpressed as the final recruit took his seat. "I really was hoping for better. Only two of you show any promise of mastering Earth, and even then, I am highly doubtful that any of you will."

Hatt looked around at the recruits and stared at them one by one. James noticed Stevie shiver after he looked her way. He then stepped forward to add to what Vask had said, "The Controller takes a special interest in the Whiteflyers coming from London, because as you know that is where he was born on Persavius. You must do better. I have no desire to cut more of you before the end of your training, but if I don't start to see progress, I will have to insist on it. Motivation is the key to success."

Not for the first time, the recruits went to sleep that night doubting whether they'd make Whiteflyer status at all. While James was fairly certain that he would be okay, he still had Stevie to worry about. He was worrying about her a lot lately, much more than he had ever worried about his friends on Earth. He had to constantly remind himself that they weren't under the usual circumstances on Torpor, and if his friends had been in the same danger that Stevie was in now, he'd feel the exact same way. As James repeatedly told himself this, his eyes went heavy and slowly he felt himself drift off to another time. A time when he was still with Liza. One where he lived with his mum and dad and where his sister visited him on long weekends. For what felt like only moments, he was oblivious to reality before he became slowly aware that someone was standing over his bed, shaking him gently and whispering in his ear.

Not letting a repeat of the night Matthew, Tim and Rufus hijacked him from his bed happen again, James sprang up, his eyes wide. He struggled to get his bearings as quickly as possible, ready to defend himself, but it was all unnecessary. Two brown eyes stared back at him, eyes too beautiful and caring to belong to anyone he hated. "Stevie, what are you doing? Is everything okay?" he urged, looking around to find out if there was an obvious reason that she was shaking him awake so late at night.

"Yeah everything is perfect but get up. I have somewhere I want to take you."

"Take me? Are you mad it's the middle of the night? We can't leave," James whispered, looking around again to make sure everyone was asleep, and nobody could hear them.

"You heard Vask on the first day. There are only two rules, so as long as we don't get into a fight on our travels or get lost and miss training tomorrow, we are all good," Stevie replied, pulling his duvet off and handing him his shoes.

"I don't mean we aren't allowed leave. I mean we can't. The door's locked."

Stevie laughed and dragged him out the door, ignoring his gentle resistance, "Ah yes you're right. It's a pity we can't move the air or anything, that way we could just unlock it."

When they got out to the door, Stevie unlocked it as easily as if they had the key. James was shocked it worked, he assumed there was some other weird magic keeping them in there. Even Stevie looked slightly surprised, "Well that's a relief. I was acting confident back there, but I was secretly unsure whether or not it would open. I guess they don't mind us going for a wander after all." James shook his head but followed Stevie outside anyway. He was never one to follow the rules and he was quite intrigued as to where she was bringing him. At first, he thought she might just want to explore the headquarters, but then he started to get excited that she'd found something, maybe even the way to get to Arcadius and Tartarus.

Just as he went to ask her where she was taking him, they arrived into the headquarters' domed entrance and he immediately realised they weren't going to stay indoors, "So when you said you wanted to take me somewhere, you really meant take me somewhere."

"Of course I did, we need some air, and not just training ground air. We haven't left this building in weeks. It's time we had some fun." James had to agree, while training distracted him a good deal, he couldn't deny that he missed exploring Torpor with Stevie, just like they had done when they first arrived there. They deserved to stretch their legs.

"Where are you bringing me?" James asked for the fifth time since they'd left the headquarters.

"You really don't take surprises well, do you?" Stevie replied, shaking her head in disbelief. "If you must know, I'm taking you to the place I used to go on Earth whenever I wanted to be alone. Nobody's ever come with me, but I reckon because we're in Torpor now I can show you. It's not technically the same place. Is It?" Stevie didn't really talk about personal things too much. She went into great detail about the escapades she'd been on and the places she'd seen, but other than when she had told James about her mum and her uncle, she kept a lot of the more personal stuff to herself. James couldn't even recall her mentioning any friends or former boyfriends. The fact she was bringing him to her special place was a big step in their friendship.

Not long after Stevie gave James an insight into where she was taking him, she finally halted. They had arrived at the River Thames just next to Albert Bridge. James had crossed the same bridge hundreds of times and he couldn't possibly imagine why anyone would use it as a place to get away from everything, for whenever he'd been there it was jam packed with lines of cars and hurried passers-by. He could even recall being run over by an angry cyclist a few years ago, just across the road from the spot they were standing.

"Well, this is… unexpected," James stated, looking around in a confused manner at the empty lit up streets.

"Not here, you moron. Down there," Stevie replied, grabbing hold of his arm and dragging him behind her for the second time that night.

"Down where?" James replied, when they had gotten to the river's edge. "Surely your thinking space isn't in the river. Is it?"

"No, obviously not. Just relax and follow my lead." As Stevie said the last two words she unexpectedly hoisted her body onto the wall of the bridge and disappeared over the other side. James' face dropped before he lunged himself forward, peering over the side of the wall. Thankfully, Stevie hadn't gone for a swim after all and instead was sitting in a small alcove carved into the side of the bridge, just under where James stood. She was smiling mischievously up at him and dangling her feet freely over the running water. "What's taking you so long? Get down here," she ordered, before James quickly followed.

"Even though we are only metres away from multiple roads, I can see why you came here, even when there would have been hundreds of cars and people passing," James said quietly, not wanting to break the mellow mood.

"Yeah it's even better with the people about. Nobody can see me, but I can watch them. The cars just become white noise," Stevie replied, keeping with the same low tone. "I found it the night my mum died. I needed to be away from the world, but part of it at the same time. This is the perfect mix."

James felt that Stevie wasn't finished so stayed silent and let her speak at her own pace. "My uncle tried his best, and he was good at being a dad, but he was a pilot, so he was gone away a lot. I suppose he thought I would get used to being alone and that I wouldn't mind it, but I didn't really like being by myself. I overthink too much. So, instead I would come out here and distract myself with the world. I had friends, don't get me wrong, but I always felt different to them. Everyone I went to school with came from rich families with a long line of wealth and influence. I felt like a bit of an imposter. My uncle had money, but my mum couldn't have been further from the type of person they'd usually associate with, so I hid my reality from them, and it ate me up inside. I couldn't be myself. It wasn't their fault of course, I never gave them the chance to accept the real me. Looking back, I should have, but analysing a situation from the outside is never really the same as living it. Is it?"

James knew how she felt. He had Liza, Jen, his friends and his parents, but sometimes he needed to be away from everything too. "Mine was my roof," James revealed when he was sure Stevie was finished. "I'd even bring binoculars up sometimes so I could fully immerse myself in other people's lives."

Stevie looked amused. "I didn't take you for the neighbour's peeping Tom," she exclaimed, pretending to be utterly offended.

James nudged her, embarrassed, "It wasn't like that. It's hard to explain. It was like plunging into a great book, but this book was real, and I knew the characters. I suppose it was like really shitty reality TV."

"I'm kidding. Who am I to judge? I spent my nights like the troll in my childhood books, hiding under a bridge," Stevie replied, almost relieved that James was just as strange as she was.

Stevie and James spent the next while trying to one-up each other with their best people watching stories. Stevie was sure that she'd win the most scandalous tale after recalling seeing a group of friends going skinny dipping after a few too many drinks, but James spying his neighbour Mrs Green having an affair with a younger man took the trophy. Stevie definitely won the funniest moment with her endless road rage encounters. One she even videoed and experienced fifteen minutes of fame on the internet with when it went viral around London. James vividly remembered seeing the video online of the old man get out of his just as old gold Buick, only to repeatedly whack the motorbike that had been tailgating him with a crowbar. The biker, both dumbfounded and furious, couldn't see how to end the situation without putting his hand on the fragile looking pensioner.

After they were all storied out, James opened his mouth to suggest getting a move on back to the headquarters to ensure they were back in bed before the morning bell, but Stevie, sensing what was coming, beat him to it. "This is where it happened," she mumbled just clearly enough for James to hear. "This is where I died." James remembered back to when he first met her, she had avoided the subject completely. He'd wondered a few times since then, but never dreamed of pushing her to tell him how she ended up in Torpor. It was her story to share. "My uncle had been gone for a week on a long-haul flight. I just remember feeling completely alone. It was lashing rain and the wind was really strong, but I didn't care. I had to get out of my house." Stevie paused for a while, she seemed unsure of how to continue but eventually carried on, "I just wanted to break free from everything, so I jumped."

James stared at her in shock, it was the very last way he'd imagined her die. "You killed yourself?" he asked, before he realised what he was saying out loud.

"No, I didn't. I didn't mean to die. I just wanted to feel the cold water on my skin, to distract myself, but the rain was too heavy, and I couldn't keep hold of the banks of the river. It's all a bit of a blur after that, but I must have drowned. I guess someone saw me fall and called an ambulance. The next thing I remember was waking up to you in the ICU. I still go to sleep at night wondering what my uncle must be thinking. All of the signs would have pointed to me wanting to have died. He will blame himself and he was nothing but amazing to me."

James didn't know what to say, he believed her that it was an accident, she wouldn't have told him anything if she didn't want to tell it in full, but it was a sad way to go all the same. James used his hideaway to get away from the hustle and bustle of life, to avoid the people he loved, but Stevie's was used for just the opposite, she wanted to feel a part of it. "I'm sorry Stevie. If I knew you on Earth, you would have had me to talk to, but you have me now and I'm not going anywhere," James assured her, reaching a rare arm around her shoulders and pulling her into a hug. He wasn't usually a hugger, but it felt nice. It felt like home. Breaking away from each other, James glimpsed a tear fall from Stevie's right eye and he immediately knew what he said was true. He was going to protect her. He wouldn't let anything bad happen to her again.

The brass bell rang loud just as James and Stevie closed their eyes in a hasty effort to pretend that they hadn't left their bed. Stevie made an overdramatic effort to stretch and yawn to hit it home in case any of their oblivious roommates suspected anything. James smiled to himself and followed suit for the fun of it. He was sure nobody noticed, or cared at that, but there was something exciting about the adventures of the night before that he wasn't ready to let go of just yet.

"I think we got away with it," Stevie uttered into James' ear, yawning simultaneously as they waited for the drudge to come and collect them for the second section of their training. From now on they'd go through all four powers every day until the competition that would announce who the chosen ten newest Whiteflyers were.

"I don't know. I think I overheard Matthew and Tim saying something about how they were going to tell Vask about empty beds and people going missing in the middle of the night," James teased, laughing at the second of worry that appeared on Stevie's face before she realised he was joking.

That morning, the drudge who escorted them out to the awaiting Whiteflyers was the older woman that had at first reminded James of Anne. Looking at her up closely, his opinion changed, and he could now see why she applied to work for The Controller in the first place. Her eyes didn't portray the honest nature of his family home's occupant and instead seemed cold and almost angry. When they got out to the oval, the woman dressed in black did not return inside as the drudges usually did, but instead walked straight up to Vask and, in a low voice that James couldn't make out, reported something. Whatever was said was short and to the point and was acknowledged only by a head nod. James felt an unsettling twitch crawl up his neck but didn't point out this new development to Stevie who was oblivious to the situation. She was in deep conversation with Annabelle about what countries they were going to fly to once they were given the all clear to keep their powers.

"Are your sleeping arrangements not good enough for you?" Vask asked the lined-up recruits, in a mock caring tone. Unsure of what he was talking about, nobody dared answer in case they misunderstood. "Or is it a holiday you are after? Or maybe you just think that you don't need to come to training well rested and alert. I for one don't see anyone before me that is proficient enough to deserve the honour of a night off, but please step forward and prove me wrong." It took everything he had, but James resisted glancing at Stevie. Vask was addressing the group as a whole, so there was still a chance he didn't know that it was Stevie and himself that had left. He didn't want to blow their cover for a comforting look. "Someone, and not a very bright someone at that, left the room last night. The door was left locked when you were dropped back to your room yesterday and when the drudge that brought you here this morning arrived to you, the lock had been opened." James cursed himself for forgetting. How could he be so stupid? He was too busy trying to hurry back into bed to remember to relock the door. "Step forward if it was you."

When nobody stepped forward, Vask repeated himself, this time louder and with more authority, "Step forward if it was you." Once again nobody stepped forward and the recruit's heads started to turn, looking up and down the line trying to source the culprit. To find the person, or people, who would be reckless enough to leave. James used the opportunity to send a message to Stevie who was standing five people away from his left. As subtly as he could, looking straight into her fearful eyes, he gently shook his head to the left and then to the right. Telling her over and over in his head, hoping she could somehow read his mind like she seemed to so many times before, not to move. Not to admit it was her. Vask had never said it was against the rules to leave their room at night, and even though James would deny his guilt to the end, the locked door was evidence enough that it shouldn't be attempted.

When nobody moved towards the furious Whiteflyer, he repeated himself for the last time. This time, forcing the air to unite his voice with each of their ears, "STEP FORWARD IF IT WAS YOU." James held his breath, silently hoping beyond despair that Stevie wouldn't give into the intimidation and give herself up, but seconds and then minutes passed, and nobody obeyed their leader's command. "Okay if the person or persons cowardly refuse to admit to their wrongdoing I am forced to believe that it was every one of you. Since you insist that you are strong enough to train without sleep, nobody is leaving this oval until I say so." The look in Vask's eyed ensured that nobody, not even Tim who could sleep for Torpor, muttered even a groan of resistance. James could feel himself getting tired even thinking about it, but he'd stay awake for the rest of the week if it meant he and Stevie would not be stopped from becoming Whiteflyers.

For the rest of the day, the recruits were taken through hoops by the Whiteflyers in an attempt by Vask to demonstrate who was in control. Anybody that hesitated or took a moment's rest was made an example of. Tim was the first person to slip up and was repeatedly blasted with water by Black until he was satisfied that he could block the blows using air. Marcus wasn't as fortunate and had his clothes set on fire when Charlie caught him yawning. Luckily, James managed to put the flames out without anyone noticing that it was him extinguishing them instead of Marcus, and he only suffered light burns that would quickly heal. Unsurprisingly, Stevie was targeted as night took over from day and her tiredness began to really kick in. She was made to float in the air as the other recruits shot fire under her feet. If she dropped, she would be burnt. James, Annabelle and

Marcus aimed their fire throws slightly off, so they'd just miss her if she dropped, but Matthew, Rowe and some others delighted in scaring her and just missed her feet by a finger's width.

By the time Vask had called it quits for the day, the other Whiteflyers had turned snarky. They'd been involuntarily assigned to work overtime at the fault of James and Stevie's outing, and weren't happy about it. Even a normally upbeat Watson snapped at them, in need of a long night's sleep. However, fortunately for them, their shifts would be swapped over the following day. Unfortunately for the recruits, they'd only get a few minutes sleep before the bell called them to wake up for the next day of training.

"I guess we won't be able to go on anymore midnight adventures until we're made Whiteflyers," Stevie whispered to James as they exhaustedly climbed into bed. "It looks like we will have to wait before we get the chance to climb onto your rooftop and spy on your neighbours," she added, happily recalling James' revelation from the night before.

"I guess not, and I might not agree in the morning, but right now, I still say it was worth it," James faintly replied, yawning into his pillow and falling into a deep dreamless sleep.

11. "THEY'RE GETTING SCARED."

The next two weeks went by a lot more smoothly than the first day of the recruit's advanced training. Every day, they were split into groups of four and rotated between Air, Fire, Water, and Earth. The Whiteflyers were able to spend a lot more time on each person's individual skill level and so James was finding it a lot easier to progress his powers. While the basic classes had been useful, he found the pace the Whiteflyers went at far too slow. Stevie was also showing huge signs of improvement, particularly with Air and Fire, and by the end of the week, she was even able to throw a fireball at one of the target boards. The only issue was that even though James and Stevie were accomplishing so much, the other recruits were also progressing at the same pace. Well at the same pace as Stevie anyway. James was top of the class by a long shot and had advanced through eighteen of the twenty-three Earth materials. Even Vask offered a proud nod or an impressed smile here and there. Matthew was the only one that was even close to taking the top spot from him but even then, at this rate, that seemed highly unlikely.

Practical training weren't the only classes proving interesting and Catherine Avery had two more very insightful history lessons, illustrating how and why the residents were split between the islands. In her own words, "Not everyone settled into the Three Worlds as well as they should have. They were too naive and ignorant to realise what would have happened if the endless ability to bear children was not stopped. The rebellions only got worse with people demanding they get their 'rights' back. The Controller watched on as innocent people were tortured and brutalised by these rebels, and as the lands he'd created were ruthlessly destroyed, he was forced to come to the conclusion that not every citizen deserved the same privileges. He couldn't be everywhere at once and so the only solution was to split the people up between the Three Worlds. The good and bad would no longer be forced to live amongst one another. Initially this was done in real time and people were moved between the worlds as and when they showed their true colours, but this was tedious, and it was later decided to give Earth another task. It was to become the testing ground for the newly born's morals.

"By this point, the majority of people had been misusing their powers solely for personal gain and to take down the society that The Controller and his followers had worked so hard to build. The only way to prevent the worlds from crumbling completely was to relinquish the power from those who insisted on using Air, Fire, Water and Earth for selfish gains. The Controller spent years travelling from world to world seeking out and drawing the power from the unworthy. Only those in his inner circle could be trusted to handle the four powers in a way that would benefit the greater good. He named these individuals the Whiteflyers. They were chosen from the most powerful and honourable of The Controller's followers, by the competition process that is still in use today. The gateways linking the Three Worlds together were destroyed and new paths that only the Whiteflyers and The Controller himself knew about, and were able to travel between, were created.

"Unrest quickly jumped to an all-time high as families and friends were separated. Tartarus, housing the worst of the world, turned into a burnt wasteland, something The Controller chose not to rebuild. It is a constant reminder to its residents that they brought their suffering on themselves. Torpor and Arcadius also suffered hugely but the reactions were not as violent and were short lived. Once the Whiteflyers got the worlds in order, The Controller rebuilt the lands as they are today. He often updates and moulds them as Earth changes, but as you will definitely have noticed from Torpor, and the successful will further notice in Arcadius, neither is a direct translation of the planet you grew up on." While Stevie and James soaked up everything that Catherine explained about the history of the worlds, her account held too many inconsistencies and contradictions, and they soon realised that the real story may have been a lot different than the one currently being taught to them. While history had a way of changing over time, something told them that in this case, the alterations hadn't occurred naturally.

"He stole their powers," Stevie voiced as they practiced their skills into the night at the beginning of the next week. James had been insisting they put double the amount of time into training as they had been the weeks before. He was growing concerned that he would be separated from Stevie in the coming weeks and was determined to not let his anxieties turn into a reality. "They are playing it off like it had to be done or we would have all been killed off, but I bet he just wanted full control over the powers. All of this time we've been told that The Controller is giving us access to the four powers, but all he is doing is giving ours back. I've read ahead in the history books and the discrepancies I've been noticing aren't clearing up. If anything, they are further proof that they are just trying to confuse us into believing their account of how and why things happened."

James had been thinking along the same lines. No matter what direction his thought process went in, it was the only logical explanation. "I remember on our first day of training when we got our powers. It felt like something I was missing had finally returned and even now they feel completely a part of me. My power source is just as much at home inside of me as my leg is attached to me. The more we practice, the more it becomes like second nature. We shouldn't be separated from them. If people were revolting, I imagine it was for a just reason. They were facing the most powerful oppressor to ever live after all," James shared.

Stevie nodded eagerly in agreement, her face scrunched up in what James wasn't sure was frustration or deep thought, "We should have been using them since we were kids. While we were learning to walk and talk, we would also have been learning to move water and conjure fire."

While it was fun to talk about overthrowing the hierarchy and restoring the residents of Arcadius, Torpor and Tartarus with their rightful powers, James wasn't taking it all too seriously just yet. After all, they were only two teenagers, new to their powers, up against the most powerful people in the world. That day may come, but in the meantime, the problem that had been playing on James' mind the most was one that he could more easily picture resulting in a happy ending. Finding Liza was the reason he wanted to become a Whiteflyer in the first place and it had to be made an immediate priority.

Over the next few weeks, James refrained from talking about Liza to Stevie as much as he could. Not because he thought Stevie minded, but because he didn't want to mix the two. Stevie was just a friend and he knew that, but Liza might not see it the same way. On Earth, James hadn't had many friends that were girls, but he did get some extra attention from some of them at school and, not that Liza was the insane jealous type, but she didn't exactly respond well to it. Going from past experience, he couldn't imagine she'd be all too pleased to meet his new best friend, especially if he was to find her alone in Tartarus. He never really thought of what he would do when the time came, but he did know that cutting Stevie out wasn't an option. He promised her he wouldn't abandon her and he intended to keep that promise.

How James was going to find Liza was still a puzzle, but the closer he came to becoming a Whiteflyer the easier he imagined it would be. After Catherine explained how there were pathways between the worlds that only The Controller and the Whiteflyers could access, he assumed it wouldn't be too difficult to come up with a reason as to why he wanted to explore Arcadius and Tartarus. He was sure that most new Whiteflyers would want to, and once he found her, he could sneak her back into Torpor with him. There were millions of people in the city he resided in, one more was sure to go unnoticed, or two if he included Stevie's mum which he almost always did when he daydreamed of reuniting with his girlfriend.

On the morning of the final day of the second last week, the drudge that was due to bring them to practice instead escorted them into the domed entrance of the headquarters. This was the second time since becoming a recruit that they were made to take part in the weekly announcements that Hatt gave to the Torpor Residents. James cringed remembering the first time he had stood on the raised entrance, eyeing a very confused Anne in the audience. This time he vowed to look ahead and avoid any contact with the people below him. He couldn't contemplate a second unexplained encounter.

After the regular information and updates were announced, and the newest Torpor residents were made known, Hatt revealed the reason the recruits had to endure this particular superiority performance, "Before you, I give you the final seventy people that will be taking part in this year's Whiteflyer's Challenge. These represent the bravest and most loyal amongst you. Ten of them will walk away with the privilege of becoming the newest Whiteflyers. For the first time, with the permission of The Controller himself, I am granting you the opportunity to witness the competition for yourselves. It will give you a small insight into what you will learn if you decide to drop the cowardice and sign up to become a Whiteflyer yourself next year."

James, along with a few others beside him, whipped his head towards Hatt in shock. Only the Whiteflyers were supposed to be in attendance at the competition. The thought of parading himself around in front of anyone else made his insides squirm. What would Anne and Tracey think? What impression would he make on everyone in Torpor that he hadn't had the opportunity to meet yet? "Share the word. The first 60,000 people registered on the day will get to witness the event in person. Televisions will be resurrected for those who do not make it. This is an event for all. It is a privilege granted to you by The Controller and it is one that you should be ever thankful for. Educational, yet exhilarating entertainment like this has not come around before and depending on how everything goes, it may never come around again."

After the announcement, the recruits walked into the training oval, noisily discussing the latest news, to the second surprise of the day. This one, not so daunting. "Today will be taken up with a series of tests designed to discover your weaknesses. It will show you the areas you need to work on and practice towards for the final week. The ten people who I, and the other Whiteflyers, feel perform the best will get a special prize this evening. Those not chosen should start to grow worried. There is only one week left to prove yourselves," Vask declared, to a nervous yet excited chatter.

For the special lesson, the training grounds were laid out differently to usual. The four training grounds were replaced with sand and only a small area, in the very centre of the grounds, held the equipment and materials needed for the recruits to showcase their raw talent.

One pool of water, one target board, and one slab containing a mix of all of the minerals, stones, and soils they had been working with in Earth training. On the far side of the display, benches made of stone were constructed from the ground for the waiting recruits and Whiteflyers to witness each person's performance.

"One by one, I want you to control your powers to mimic what I am asking you to do. These commands will start off basic and progress as your power levels are tested," Vask explained as everyone took their seats and anxiously waited to be called upon. "The performances here will give everyone a very good idea of who could be chosen the week after." While they wouldn't know exactly what they were to expect the following week, James guessed that if they weren't able to do the basic manoeuvres that Vask called out at the beginning of each person's turn, they would have little to no chance of making it into the top ten in the class.

Alphabetically, the recruits went up and performed as well as they could. The pressure weighed heavy, but it was nothing compared to what they'd have to go through during the real thing so both James and Stevie welcomed the rehearsal of sorts. Thousands of eyes would be on them the following week, most of them James imagined, hoping that they would fail. At the end of the day and when everyone had completed what had been asked of them to the best of their abilities, the recruits lined up and waited as the Whiteflyers decided on their verdict and Vask announced the chosen ten.

"If your name is called out, please step forward; James Moore, Matthew Avery, Annabelle White, Tessa Higgins, Dennis Reilly, Paul Willis, Rufus Martin, Rowena Daley, Alex Mitchell, and lastly, Stevie Miller."

James' heart exploded when he heard Stevie's name being called out. Depending on the day, and from his own assessments, she had been jumping in and out of the top ten. To avoid gloating loudly, he squeezed her hand to let her know that he was just as happy as she must be feeling, but Stevie didn't show the same restraint and yelped loudly, "Yes, I knew I could do it!", before realising what James had moments before.

She quietly looked down at the floor and James whispered back, "I knew you could too. One more week of training twice as hard as everyone else and we should both be guaranteed a place."

That night a drudge arrived to bring the recruits to take part in the surprise they'd been promised. They had all been excitedly discussing what they might be doing for it since leaving the oval. The reassurance that they could all possibly be made Whiteflyers the following week was enough to even calm the tension between Matthew and James for one evening. Another movie was off the cards when the drudge bypassed the cinema room and instead brought them into a room they'd only passed through before; the music room. The room looked bigger than it had previously, and James guessed that that was because it was. One of the level four Whiteflyers, most likely, had temporarily expanded it to fit the hundreds of chairs that looked onto a low platform where a piano took centre stage. The drudge ushered them towards the seats at the back of the room and, before long, the wonder of who would be filling the vacant places was cleared up, as Whiteflyers began to stream into the room. Some who James knew personally by now, others who he had never so much as seen from a distance.

A while after everyone had taken their seats, Hatt graced the stage, "Settle down, settle down! While it's not rare that we all come together to socialise, it's rare we let anyone else join us. On this occasion, we decided to make an exception for the ten recruits at the back of the room. With only a week to go until our numbers increase, we thought a snippet of what is to come will only serve to motivate you all to do your very best at the final competition." As everyone turned towards the back of the room, James started to grow hot, but just as quickly and with little reaction, they turned back to Hatt as he continued, "Tonight we have an extra special performance from someone with bundles of talents. A musician whose useless talents in other areas of her life, proved to be for the best." Just then, with an outstretched hand from Hatt, a figure appeared through the door. James' face dropped as the musician, cloaked in the drudge's blacks, walked in. It was Rebecca. To James' surprise her skin was free from the telling scars he expected to find after such an ordeal. On Earth, the scorching would have killed her, but on Torpor, no reminder was evident on her body.

"Is this a sick joke?" Stevie asked, louder than she should have, but quiet enough for only the other recruits to hear.

Rowe shot her head around to answer, uncaring that the question was not directed at her. "I don't see the problem Miller. She's going to play the piano. A talent the Whiteflyers can actually use. I'd imagine your fate won't be as easy, you don't seem like the kind who can do anything unique. Actually, if I am honest, I am shocked that you are here at all. You were last to be read out on the list, so I imagine you just scraped your way through. I can't foresee the same happening next week, so I'd try to enjoy the music instead of spending your time whining. Or maybe you think Rebecca will give you a solo concert when you join her next week, so you don't see the point. If so, I highly doubt they have pianos in your new living quarters, so I wouldn't hold your breath if I was you." James took hold of Stevie's arm and urged her not to retaliate, there were too many Whiteflyers around to risk causing a scene. They were nearly at the finish line. They had to remain calm until they were granted the only thing that stood any chance of beating them, their powers. Reluctantly, she inhaled a deep gulp of air and silently agreed, turning her attention back to the stage.

As Rebecca began to play, James tried his best not to enjoy the performance. It wasn't right that she was being forced to entertain the very people who had done such cruel things to her not so long ago, but the sound was unlike anything he had ever heard. He didn't know if she was just that good or if the absence of any music at all heightened his appreciation for it. Classical music wasn't his usual preference, but the sounds of the violin transported him back to Ireland to his granny's house. The song Rebecca was playing was from a favourite movie of hers that was usually reserved for Christmas time in most households but would often play in the background during any season of the year as his granny went about her business. James felt a pang of sadness in his stomach, realising that Christmas was probably now a thing of the past. Maybe they had it in Arcadius, but he couldn't imagine the people of Torpor celebrating such a joyous festival.

When Rebecca finished three and then four songs, she took a bow and went to leave the stage before another drudge entered, this one holding a violin. After him, a drudge that could sing finished off the evening with some more modern songs that James could sing along to in his head. James felt guilty as they got up to follow the same drudge that had been playing the violin back to their quarters, as if he hadn't already done enough service for them in one night. "Why the long face Moore?" Matthew asked, shoving his shoulder into James' back as he walked into their bedroom. "Don't forget that they signed up for it. Just as all of these other losers did," he added, pointing his hands out at the recruits that weren't chosen to watch the show.

As Matthew's finger pointed in Marcus' direction, Marcus immediately jumped down from the bunk bed and marched towards him. His eyes on fire. "I wouldn't underestimate me, Avery. You don't know who you're dealing with," he expressed, pushing his forehead against Matthew's face. "Don't touch me Marcus. I will make your life a living hell by the end of next week," Matthew threatened, conjuring a small ball of fire in his hand.

James jumped in and grabbed Marcus by the chest, pushing him back before anything could escalate further. Matthew was a lot more powerful than Marcus and this wouldn't end well for anyone if the former's threats proved to hold substance. "I could take him James. You're not the only one with powers around here. This is bullshit," Marcus yelled angrily, punching his bed as he hopped back on and turned away from the onlookers. "I know you could mate, but it wouldn't prove anything. It would just put you on the wrong side of Vask if the room was burnt up," James lied, knowing deep down that Marcus was no match for Matthew when it came to the four powers.

"They're getting scared. We all are," Stevie whispered to James as they drifted off to sleep not long after the confrontation. "I know I made the cut today, but Rowe was right, it was a close call. I still have a lot of work to do this week if I'm going to make it a reality."
"We will work all night, every night if we have to. We are both coming out as Whiteflyers at the end of this. I promise," James reassured her, meaning every word. "Now go to sleep. It starts tomorrow."

12. "IT'S COMPETITION DAY."

The night before their final class with Catherine Avery, where James and the others would have to write an essay on everything they had learned about the history of the worlds, James and Stevie sat in the lounge area quizzing each other back and forth. They needed to know about Persavius, The Controllers early life, and the creation of the Three Worlds, but also about the different influential Whiteflyers that had come before them. It was easy to remember enough about the faces hanging in their own training room. The majority they had met, some had even taught them, but learning about the well known Whiteflyers on Arcadius and Tartarus wasn't as painless. Arcadius was home to nineteen Whiteflyers who had mastered all four power levels and Tartarus was home to seventeen, so they substantially increased the amount of information they had to store in their memory.

"I hate written exams," James complained, not for the first time that night. "I want to get back to practical training. Even though I've learnt to control all of the Earth materials, I haven't spent nearly enough time on the mixed Earth box and that's the most important one. If I want to spend my last two days focusing solely on that in training during the day, I need to make sure I am giving enough attention to Air, Fire and Water at night."

Stevie rolled her eyes and shook her head, "You're the last person in the room who should be complaining about not being prepared enough for Sunday. You're just bored."

James reluctantly had to agree. Studying from books brought him back to school and reminded him of some of the awful teachers he had experienced over the years. Once his French teacher refused to acknowledge his existence until he was forced to move subjects. He had never known her to be so friendly as the day he told her it was his last. "That's for the best James, Spanish might be more suited to you. French just isn't your subject," she had said, feigning concern for his future. They weren't all bad though, some of them actually cared, but it was hard to solely remember them when the pretentious ones were so arrogant and patronising.

"Fine. It's getting late anyway. I suppose we've done all we can for now. Let's get a good night's sleep, we haven't had much this week with all the extra practice you're making us do," Stevie conceded not long after James started staring at her unblinking with a turned down face until she was forced to give in.

"Everybody put your books away. If you haven't studied enough by now, I am afraid it is too late," Catherine Avery announced from the top of her classroom the following morning. "Write as much about what you have learnt to date as you can until the sundial's shadow reaches here," she explained pointing to an old stone device that none of the recruits had ever seen before.

"And this is why we need watches," Marcus complained to Stevie and James. "I can't even see that."

"I will give you ample warning Mr Davis. You should have plenty of time," Catherine replied unexpectedly, as James opened his mouth to agree. Embarrassed that she overheard him, Marcus nodded his acceptance eagerly before pointing his head down towards the blank pages in front of him as if he was reading a question sheet.

"You may begin."

"Well that wasn't hard at all," Stevie told an agreeable Annabelle on their way out to the training oval after the essay. "I'm pretty sure I remembered everything important. I thought she'd ask some questions, but I guess they think our own account of what we have learnt would be less leading." James who was listening from behind couldn't have disagreed more. How was he supposed to know what they wanted from him if there were no questions? He'd glanced over at Stevie's desk near the end of the allocated time and it looked as though she had filled nearly twice the number of pages as he had. He was bound to have missed more than one or two vital bits of history. If he was being compared to her, he couldn't imagine Catherine would grade him very well. Marcus, who walked alongside James, seemed just as disappointed. Matthew on the other hand, looked extremely pleased with himself. There was no way he would have let himself down in front of Catherine, and unless it was while James slept, he didn't come to bed the night before. From the look on Tim's face, he didn't share in his best friend's satisfaction.

James shook off his displeasure and pushed the essay from his mind completely. What was done was done and now it was time to put everything he had into the last two days of practice. Stevie was the one who really needed to do well in the essay out of the two of them anyway, and as far as she was concerned, she'd aced it. After all, Vask had said it was mainly used to decide between people who had performed similarly in the main competition, and if Stevie was currently in tenth place, it would push anyone gaining on her back a few steps.

"As there are only one and a half days of training left, everyone is free to practice any area that they please. The other Whiteflyers and I will be walking around to assist where we are needed," Vask announced to the lined up recruits. "I would strongly recommend that you work on the areas that were flagged to you during last week's challenge. There is no room for fancy demonstrations of your powers if you can't get the fundamentals one hundred percent right." Stevie took his advice and headed straight to the Air practice grounds to get a firmer hold of the basics. James, who was practically fluent in Air, Fire and Water by now headed to Earth to practice manipulating more than one element together.

The night before the competition, the recruits gathered in their living area to listen to Elizabeth, Watson, Charlie, Alton, Joseph, and Alice, who had taken centre stage to walk them through any last minute tips they were allowed to give. While they weren't able to reveal what would be asked of them the following day, they were able to give them a better insight into how the day would proceed. "Nobody will be able to watch anyone who goes before them. It would be an unfair advantage to let you familiarise yourself with the course before your turn comes around and it would possibly even give you the opportunity to steal other people's moves," Watson explained to the room full of eagerly listening recruits who were hanging onto his every word. "Once you've finished, you can take a seat and witness the remainder of the competition."

James hadn't really thought about whether or not he'd be able to watch everyone else's turn. He was allowed to watch the practice round the week before, so he'd been picturing a similar set up to that. It would be nice to know where he and Stevie stood before the results were read out, but he supposed the rule made sense to avoid giving anyone any advantages. "After each person has completed the course, they will be rated by all of the Whiteflyers. Vask, Hatt and Catherine's votes will hold the most authority. The ten chosen and, therefore, the newest Whiteflyers will be announced at a ceremony at the end," Elizabeth interrupted James' thought process. "We, of course, didn't experience the competition with onlookers. But if anything, the atmosphere should intensify your resolve to do well."

Charlie laughed at this last sentence and added, "Unless you choke, but then again cowards don't belong as Whiteflyers, so it's best you're flushed out early." Alton started chuckling along with Charlie and even the Whiteflyers James had grown to tolerate like Alice and Watson smiled. Most of the people the Whiteflyers were addressing would end up as drudges before the next twenty-four hours were over and being a coward had absolutely nothing to do with it. While James disagreed with the majority of the recruit's motives, and while he didn't care much for most of them, he did know that there was nothing cowardly about what they had gone through over the last two months.

That night, James didn't sleep too well. A recurring nightmare, where he messed up in the challenge and didn't get picked to be a Whiteflyer, kept replaying itself in his dreams. He'd wake up in a panic after hearing Liza's screams from Tartarus, having no way to get to her. "I can't sleep either," Stevie muttered from the bed beside him after his third or fourth time replaying the dream.

"Why is it that the more you try to avoid a dream the more it makes itself at home while you sleep?" James asked, giving up on any chance of falling into a deep sleep.

Stevie shrugged, "I remember after I went to live with my uncle, I couldn't shake this nightmare that something horrible was happening to my mum. It wouldn't always start the same, but it would always end... well let's just say it would always end badly. Sometimes I would go weeks, and sometimes even months without it, but it always came back. The night before I got the news that my mum had passed away was the last time it followed me to sleep. Once it had become a reality, I stopped fearing it and the nightmares went away."

"So, what you're saying is that the only way to stop them is to live it?" James replied, wondering how that would possibly help.

"No. I am saying that the only way to stop having nightmares is to surpass the fear," Stevie corrected, as if the moral of her story had been abundantly clear.

"And here I was thinking I was brave," James joked, pretending to be insulted.

"Only those who live without love can be completely fearless," Stevie whispered back, ignoring James' sarcastic undertones.

James supposed Stevie was right, while he would consider himself brave when it came to most things, when it came to the ones he cared about, he couldn't stand the thought of them being in pain. Liza had told him before that his protectiveness was one of the main reasons that she loved him. She felt safe with him. The irony of that stung James deep in the gut. He was the one who had put her in the most danger of all and getting her out was taking a lot longer that he would have liked.

James fell back asleep one more time before finally giving up and deciding to have an early morning. A few of the other recruits had the same thought as he did, and the baths weren't as empty as he first hoped they would be. As James sunk into the hot water, he happily watched Annabelle pull spheres of water from the sudsy bath, evaporating them with the fire rising from the palm of her other hand when they got too high. Marcus anxiously sat watching, never having managed to manipulate water himself. "Are you sure you can't tell me how to do that?" he asked in a panic. "Why has nobody told me how they are doing it?"

Annabelle rolled her eyes, "You know I can't Marcus or I would have already. Anyway, Water is the last thing you need to be concentrating on at the moment. As Vask said, usually only a few of those chosen have mastered Water, the rest make do with Fire and Air, so you should be concentrating on what you know. It's competition day. Nothing new will be useful to you this late on." While James couldn't help but agree with Annabelle, he knew why Marcus was so eager to learn what he could at the last minute. He was only ever picked in the top ten of the recruits once, and that was weeks ago. James knew that if he was in the same position, he would also be desperately trying to pull something out of the bag that would push him over the edge.

James decided against practicing anything. He was confident enough with every power bar Earth and there were no training materials for it in their common area. Either way, he was never the kind to have rehearsed before a presentation, or he would second guess himself and mess up during the real thing. Just as he stood to get out of the bath and wait for the drudge to bring them out to their destiny, he felt two hands lean onto his shoulders. A flash of Matthew, Tim and Rufus' attempt to drown him flooded his brain and he violently grabbed hold of both the forearms pushing on his shoulders, readying himself to burn whoever it was that stood behind him. However, just before he released the hot energy that was building up inside of him, he stuttered. The arm he was holding was a lot thinner than he'd imagined either of his enemies to be and it was a lot smoother, with very little hair. "Ow, what the Tartarus do you think you're doing?" Stevie yelped, trying to break free from James' tight grasp.

James released her immediately and whisked around, fear filling his face. "Stevie. It's you. I nearly…" but before he could finish Stevie did, "You nearly broke my arm, that's what you nearly did. Your hands were strangely hot. You weren't going to... Were you?"

James blushed and climbed onto the bathroom floor to explain himself, but when he pulled himself up, three new faces had appeared. "Trying to get rid of another girlfriend are you Moore? It's certainly not the competition you're trying to eliminate anyway. Stevie is hardly worth your energy in that department," Matthew sniggered, egged on by a chuckling Rowe and Tim beside him.

"Don't you remember what happened last time I got angry Matthew? Thanks for the ammunition for the challenge later," James replied, winking at Tim before turning his back from their dumbstruck faces.

"I can't believe it. Did James Moore just walk away from a fight?" Stevie asked, feigning surprise as they walked over to their wardrobes to get dressed.

James smiled, "I just took a leaf out of your book and thought it would be better to distract him a little, than to start a fight. Let him think I'll put on another show like I did on the last day of fire."

"Who knows, maybe you will," Stevie added, before climbing into her grey robes for the last time.

A drudge came to collect the recruits later than usual that morning. As soon as they had left their living quarters, they could hear excited chatter and loud shouts coming from the oval. As long as James had known them, the people of Torpor had never sounded even mildly enthusiastic. "Who knew they still had it in them?" Tessa said, mirroring his thoughts to no one in particular. "I guess they have just wanted something to do."

The regular pathway to their training ground was altered and the usual entrance led into a closed off room instead of out into the open. The room was fitted with a dozen long benches and tables and at the far end was a thin hallway, just wide enough for one person. It led to a door that James presumed was the oval's new temporary entrance.

"Welcome everyone. Please take your seats." Watson called from behind them. "As you can see, some minor adjustments were made to your training grounds yesterday evening. We had to make room for thousands of spectators after all, so I wouldn't expect too much familiarity when you get out there."

Alton who had come in with Watson continued, "Your practice challenge last week wasn't just for kicks. You have all been seeded for today's competition. A list has been drawn up, ranking your performances so far from worst to best. It will determine the order you will compete in." James could hear Stevie sigh a breath of relief. He himself wasn't as pleased with the order of things. He hated waiting around for things, it made him uneasy. He'd be last, and this way he wouldn't get to assess how anyone else performed. He wouldn't even be able to see Stevie compete.

"Benjamin Flynn, you're up first."

Benjamin was a small man that didn't really interact with the other recruits, and even though James had never said as much as hello to the man, he couldn't help but feel sorry for him. He was not only the first to go into the unknown, but it was with the fresh knowledge that he had performed the worst in the competition the week before. Benjamin looked shocked; it wasn't a surprise to most that he was chosen to go first but hope can have a funny way of convincing people that they're closer to their goal than they really are.

As Benjamin waited at the end of the short hallway, waiting for the doors to open to meet his fate, James could swear his legs were shaking gently. With no friends to wish him good luck and to wave him goodbye, he didn't look back as he walked out to meet the thousands of blurry faces, of whom James only got a brief glimpse at before the door was quickly closed. Roars erupted from the other side of the wall, as a muffled Vask introduced the first contestant.

"I never thought I'd agree with her, but Tessa is right, they really are in a whole different mood today," Stevie observed, nervously biting her nails between words. "Let's hope they keep up the momentum for when our turn comes around. Hopefully they don't turn sour."

"I don't know," James replied. "They don't exactly love Whiteflyers do they? I reckon a few burns and falls won't get them too worked up." Stevie didn't answer and instead ripped the tops of her nails off even more aggressively. James stared at her concerned, she needed to calm down if she was going to make it into the final ten. From past experience, she only performed well when she wasn't inside her own head.

Over the next ten minutes or so, the recruits eagerly listened as the crowd oohed, awwed, went silent and cried out, and not before long Alton came back into the room to call on the next recruit, and then the next and the next, to take their turn in the newly renovated oval. When half of the recruits had walked out the door, a silent Stevie finally spoke up, "If I don't do well. I need you to do something for me."

James cut across her before she could finish, refusing to let her stop believing in herself before the very last hurdle, "Stevie Miller. What is it you said to me after our first week of training?"

"To stop worrying and that I was going to become a Whiteflyer."

James nodded, "So then tell me why you're the only one worrying now? You believed in yourself when you were, well let's face it, not the most powerful, but now that you have proved how strong you are and exactly where you belong, you've decided that you might not be good enough. We are both going to be chosen to be Whiteflyers at the end of this, so take your fingers out of your mouth, stop jittering your legs and hold off telling me what you need me to do for you, because you are going to be around to do it for yourself." Stevie looked up, pulling her finger nails from her face and flashed the charming smile that James had now reluctantly grown to associate with a swarm of butterflies. "That's better, now let's have some fun. From the sounds of the crowd, I am pretty sure Mark just got set alight and is now waddling off to the nearest water source to put the flames out."

Stevie laughed, "No he didn't. He fell 10 feet and landed in a soil patch. He's trying to wade himself out but he can't see. There's too much mud in his eyes," she contradicted.

For the rest of the afternoon, James and Stevie narrated the scenes they could hear coming from the oval out loud to each other. The people they got on with seemed to end up a lot better off than those they didn't, with Tim even managing to burn his clothes off if Stevie's account was to be believed. But not before long the inevitable caught up to them and Watson announced that a much calmer Stevie Miller should get ready to enter the oval. "You've got this Stevie. How could they not pick you?" Annabelle whooped, as Stevie opened the door to attempt the performance of her life.

"See you on the other side Miller," James added, just before the door shut, mentally preparing himself to try to piece together, in his opinion, the most important recruit's power showcase in his head.

James could hear the crowd cheering as Stevie entered the grounds and Vask directed her to the starting point. Her deep red hair contrasting against her sallow skin made her stand out in a brilliant way and the crowd seemed to instantly warm to her. James could tell when she had started the competition; the sounds coming from the people on the other side of the wall heightened and then lowered and then sprang back up again just as fast. Judging by the amount of time the other recruits had spent in the oval, Stevie was around half way through when James heard the first sound he didn't like. The crowd oooed awkwardly as if something hadn't happened as it should have, but it wasn't long before the crowd hyped up again, cheering for her victory. The second and last uncomfortable sounds that made their way into the recruits waiting room were muffled boos that were quickly overpowered by cheers. Shortly afterwards, Watson came back into the room signalling that Stevie's turn was over and called for the next potential Whiteflyer to get ready.

Overall, James was happy with how Stevie's performance had sounded. With only two brief moments standing out negatively, he put it to the side and concentrated on his own presentations. He watched and waited, as there were only eight people, then five and then one person left before he had to take on the unexplored and hopefully come out the other side with all four powers. As Matthew was called to ready himself, James felt nerves creep up inside him for the first time that day. They reminded him of sports day at school when he was a kid. He would plead with his dad that he actually needed to go to the bathroom and that it wasn't just his nerves tricking him into thinking he did. The flashback and butterflies combined successfully ensured he zoned out for the next while and after what only seemed like a minute or two later, Watson re-entered the room to call the last person to stand. "James, you're up. My bets on you, so don't let me down," he added with a wink before exiting the back door that he had come through, where he had presumably found another way to watch the recruits in action.

As James opened the door to enter the oval as a recruit for the last time, he was blindsided by the sheer amount of faces that were staring back at him. The oval's size and shape remained intact, but huge towering stone stands had been resurrected on three of the four sides, for the onlookers to witness the spectacle from. It reminded James of a movie about gladiators he had once watched. He briefly wondered would they issue him with a thumbs up or a thumbs down by the end of his performance, before taking in the rest of the sight.

On the other side of the oval, where the headquarters sat, hundreds of grand stone chairs were propped up above the roof. This created a space, away from the boisterous crowds, for the Whiteflyers to watch and judge the performances from. As he spun in a circle, his nerves were compelled to disappear as rows and rows of blurry people cheered and chanted for him. While becoming a Whiteflyer who had access to Air, Fire, Water, and Earth would be a huge advantage if he wanted to set these people free, his drive and motivation to accomplish his goals would remain unbroken no matter how the day ended. He wouldn't stop until everyone in the oval's, and everyone who occupied the Three World's excitement at watching him use his powers had changed to excitement in using their own.

Pulling his eyes away from the bystanders, James noticed how differently the oval was laid out than he was used to. An obstacle course spanned three quarters of the open space and a blank sand pitch took up the final section. Target boards, pools of water and patches of Earth's materials littered the floor in what seemed from a first glance like a random arrangement. But before James could take it in fully, a loud voice amplified around the arena. "James Moore, take your place to the right of the course."

Turning around to see where the voice was coming from and to get a better look at the observing Whiteflyers seated atop the headquarters, James spotted the recruits seated at the back of the roof. Happiest of all, and eagerly waving and whistling at him, was Stevie. "I guess she did alright then," James mumbled to himself gleefully, before turning back around to do as Vask had asked.

When James got to a small and slightly raised black circle on the far side of the pitch he jumped onto it and combed his hands through his hair. Unsure of what he was to do next, he looked directly in front of him to try to gather his bearings. Black shiny metal pillars, ranging from one to over one hundred metres high were scattered around the first part of the pitch, but it wasn't immediately clear what James was supposed to do with them. They had been told before that they'd be given instructions on what to do, but the more James thought about it, the more he realised that he didn't hear Vask announcing directions from the waiting room for anyone else. Did they change their mind? Was he supposed to just free style through the whole thing? James glanced up at Vask hoping for some sort of signal, but when he wasn't given any he decided to try his luck and take a step off of the circle. Just as his foot was about to touch the ground, Vask began to speak into his ear, no louder than if he was standing right next to him. "Where do you think you're going Moore? I haven't told you what to do yet," Vask questioned in his usual demanding tone. James went to answer but held his tongue after remembering the communication was only one way. "Follow my instructions as you move from this side of the arena to the other. Your aim is to complete as much of it as successfully as you can. Some parts will require your imagination, for others you are to do exactly as you are told. Anything you think you can't do, can be either attempted or skipped. The last empty space is designed for freestyling. Any powers you feel you didn't get to show off to your complete potential should be concentrated on here. There's no limit to how long you spend on each obstacle, but it will be taken into account during the judging process." James took a deep breath, shook out his body, and stepped off the metal plate.

Just as his foot hit the sand in front of him, Vask gave James his first, and very brief, instruction, "Stand on as many pillars as possible." James didn't even wait for Vask to finish before he had launched himself in the air and landed safely and steadily on the first one. Flying, or hovering as Vask called it, was almost like second nature to him now. Quickly and efficiently he moved from pillar to pillar only stopping to make it known that he could. On arrival at the last and highest pillar, James couldn't help but take a moment to really reflect on everything from his aerial view. Past the buzzing stadium he could see large groups of people gathered together beside huge television screens, a vivid reminder that he was being filmed and broadcast across Torpor's London.

Arriving back to solid ground, James only had a brief moment to digest the numerous target boards positioned in multiple angles in front of him before Vask relayed his second blunt but clear instruction, "Set every target board alight." James did as he was asked and ran through the boards setting each one on fire as he passed. An eruption of cheers from the audience after every hit motivated him to move just that bit faster and in no time at all he found himself looking back at the completed task, all of the boards radiating with an orange glow. "Make it to the other side unscathed," Vask ordered before James had time to reflect on the next obstacle. Turning back around, James hesitated for the first time. The next part of the oval didn't look threatening in any way but Vasks last word implied that danger lurked ahead. Aside from the odd pool of water, the patch of land in front of him was vacant. With nothing else to do, James proceeded forward with caution, his power source ready for any unexpected trouble.

After only three or four steps James' wariness proved necessary and a ball of flame came flying from a shadowed area just off the edge of the oval. Not a moment too soon, James conjured a large gust of wind that blew out the fireball only moments before it was destined to touch skin. Ready for what was to come, James moved faster, impatient to pass this particular hurdle as quickly as possible. Fireballs came in more swiftly than he could see them, and he was forced to pre-empt where the next ones would hit. The scattered water pools came in handy and gave him the ability to get rid of multiple flames in one go, but the fire was coming towards him faster and they would eventually build up to a point where he could not get rid of them. "That's it!" James mumbled before surprising the onlookers by stopping. Concentrating everything he had on the stone beneath his feet, James manoeuvred the shape to form a wall on either side of him. As soon as the ground around his body began to rise, the flames sprang in his direction more aggressively. However, they couldn't penetrate the stone, giving him time to expand the wall to reach the other side of the obstacle. James ran swiftly and safely through his makeshift passageway unharmed before any of the hidden Whiteflyers, who were no doubt responsible for the fire, broke through.

The next problem was a lot more obvious than the previous one, and James knew what to do before he was even told. But even so, he waited for his instructions, forcing himself not to get ahead of himself. "Move the water from the pool on your right into the pool on your left," Vask directed. James, already pre-empting what he had to do, created a water stream going from one pool to the other and was onto the next obstacle within seconds. "Isolate each material from the twenty three that have been mixed into the ground in front of you," Vask ordered, as James stood at the last hurdle, before a final opportunity to freestyle. While James had worked with the mixed Earth patch before, he had never separated it out and had instead always worked with it as a whole. Kicking himself for the oversight, James cleared his head and closed his eyes, concentrating everything he had on the different ways the materials felt in practice, trying to determine which was which. The first few materials were hard to place, but the more James got into it, the easier he found his flow and not before long the crowd was cheering louder than he thought possible, as the last few materials came apart and positioned themselves away from the rest.

As James stood facing the empty sand pit, he replayed the entire challenge in his head, trying to decide what areas he didn't show off to his full potential. He'd completed everything that was asked of him, but maybe Vask and the others wouldn't agree, or maybe they still expected him to finish with a bang. Going through the tasks, James decided his safest bet was to show off all four powers. He rose into the air to begin.

The audience clapped as he flew into the sky, beckoning James to turn his attention towards them. Addressing them for the first time, "I need a volunteer," he called out, using air to extend his voice throughout the stadium. Taken off guard, having never been spoken to, everyone went silent. While the spectators enjoyed watching the four powers in use from afar, James guessed that the experiences they'd had, and the stories they'd been told about the Whiteflyers using them on the residents, rang too deep for them to want to be involved. James' stomach grew nervous, he'd gone too far to change his act now. It wouldn't be in his favour. But just then he heard it, a muffled woman calling out. The crowd around her began to yell for his attention, and it wasn't long before he had pinpointed where the volunteer was seated. Still in the air, he swiftly moved towards her, and then stopped. It was Tracey.

He hadn't seen her since he first got to Torpor, but she must have found out that he was trying to become a Whiteflyer somehow. If she hadn't seen him for herself at one of the weekly announcements,

Anne may have told her. If she was looking for him, the first place she would have checked would have been his old house, which Anne now called home. Unsure of why Tracey had come, James knew it wasn't the time for answers and he instead continued on with the act as if he didn't know her. "We have a volunteer," James declared, artificially amplifying his voice. "Please come down the stairs and out onto the arena" Tracey nodded and did as she was told, showing no sign that she was going to interrupt James' performance. "Ladies and gentlemen, today you've been given a sneak peek into what is possible when you have the power to control Air, Fire, Water and Earth. I am going to take this one step further and bestow those same powers on one of you," James shouted gleefully, getting into full character. The audience, happier than they had been for the whole performance, cheered in delight at the possibility. Before calming them down and beginning his first demonstration, James turned to Tracey and whispered, "Don't be scared. I have you." With a confirming nod, James came back to the ground and began.

"I give you Air", he yelled, at the same time lifting Tracey from the ground, giving off the illusion that she was doing it herself. Tracey embraced the role and even stretched out an arm to mimic a flying superhero. The crowd erupted in applause, imagining themselves in Tracey's position. James waited a moment before bringing her back to the ground, so the audience could fully soak-in what was happening. "Fire," he then shouted, this time even louder, while flames engulfed her stocky hands. The crowd went silent momentarily, but after realising she was in no harm, began to stamp their feet and clap. "Water," he exclaimed next, shooting a water bubble from the nearest pool. Tracey, taking the cue, opened her mouth and swallowed it. "And lastly, I give you, EARTH." As James said this, he lifted his arms dramatically into the air and with it, Tracey rose from the ground on a platform made from the stone that sat below the sand under her feet. The crowd got to their feet and the whole stadium screamed in joy. James had never felt so important in his entire life. The hope he was giving these people would not be empty. While Hatt and the other Whiteflyers would assume James' display was done in the hopes of getting the people of Torpor to sign up as recruits, the reality was that James was giving these people a foreshadow of what he was working on to restore.

Not before long, a drudge came out of the room the recruits had been using to wait for their turn and ushered James back inside. Moments later the back door opened and the rest of the recruits came rushing back to meet him. "James, you did it. You have to have got all four power levels, that was outstanding," Stevie gushed, scampering towards him. "From what I saw, you were the only one who could separate the materials." Lowering her voice, she added, "Matthew only managed a few and it took him longer than all of yours combined. And Tracey, who knew she would be here? She didn't seem angry from up close did she? Hatt looked super impressed that you involved the audience. It was the reason he decided to open up the competition to them after all. But don't think I didn't get the real meaning of your spectacle. Pure genius."

James shook his head overwhelmed and embarrassed that Stevie was bringing so much attention to him. "Relax Stevie, take a breath. Enough about me. Tell me about yours. I didn't get to see it," he asked, trying to deflect the room's energy away from himself. Everyone was staring at him, their thoughts unreadable.

"I don't want to get too excited yet, but I think it's the best I've ever performed. I got burnt a few times going through the fire balls, but most of us did. I skipped the Water and the Earth tasks obviously, which garnered a few boos, but I think I made up for it with my freestyle."

Before Stevie could go into much detail on the other performances that she witnessed, a drudge came in to collect the recruits and march them into the oval for the last time. The majority of them were pale with nerves, and a very few beamed with excitement. The only other evident emotion was anger, and Matthew was the only one who portrayed it. James guessed he didn't perform as well as he had hoped to, but at the same time he was sure that he would make the top ten.

While the recruits were waiting for the Whiteflyers to come to a conclusion, the oval had been redesigned for the second time. The pools had been filled, and the target boards and polls had been moved to the far side of the arena. They were replaced with four slightly raised platforms that Vask asked the recruits to line up behind, before Hatt began his first announcement of the day. Addressing the crowd, he began, "Today, you have witnessed what it takes to become one of us. To learn to protect the people of Torpor and to restore peace and order to our world. Even though not everyone who has performed for you today will be given the ability to move on to the next chapter in their life and become Whiteflyers, they have all proven that they have the drive and passion, if not the necessary skills. They will, however, do their part by serving The Controller and staying on in the headquarters for the next one hundred years. While this might seem daunting to most, ask yourselves, what is a mere century to someone who is destined to live forever? If it means you might get the chance to spend eternity with the gifts of Air, Fire, Water and Earth, is it not worth it?"

As Hatt's speech came to a close, Vask stepped forward to call out the list of recruits that had been chosen to swap their greys for whites. "James Moore, please step onto the first platform," Vask requested, motioning to the platform furthest to his right. James squeezed Stevie's arm and did as he was asked. "I am very pleased to announce that you were the only recruit to master all four powers, and the ninth ever level four Whiteflyer to come out of Torpor." The crowd blew up at this proclamation, clearly still filled with the hope that James' freestyle showcase had left them with. James went bright red with awkwardness, but he also felt more hopeful than he had since first coming to Torpor and realising Liza wasn't with him. Now that he could keep all four powers, it wouldn't be long before he knew she was safe.

"Matthew Avery, Annabelle White and Tessa Higgins please step up onto the second platform.", Vask requested. "You have all successfully mastered three levels of powers, Air, Fire and Water." The crowd cheered quieter than they had for James, but still made their excitement known. While James was happy Annabelle made it, he couldn't truly celebrate until he heard Stevie's name being called. He looked back at her, and her smiling face was all he needed for reassurance. "While two platforms remain, only one more will be filled. No recruit has ever before made it as a Whiteflyer without mastering at least two levels and I am happy to say this continues today. Dennis Reilly, Rowena Daley, Mary Anne Humphrey, Rufus Martin, Paul Willis, and Tim Greer, please step up onto the third platform. You have all made it as Whiteflyers."

James' face dropped to the floor as the tenth and last name was called out. It couldn't be true, they worked so hard, Stevie had to become a Whiteflyer too. Staring back at her confused face only made the lump in his stomach expand further. Only moments before she was radiantly happy, convincing him that she'd done enough. "There must be some mistake," he said loud enough for the people around him to hear. He had seen Tim in training dozens of times, and Stevie was almost always better than him. It wasn't fair.

As the residents filed out of the arena, content with the only entertaining day they'd have for at least another year, James ran towards Stevie to comfort her before she was taken away to join the other drudges. "I'm going to Vask. This isn't how it's supposed to be. We had plans together. I can't leave you to be a drudge alone. I promised I wouldn't leave you," James protested, trying to think up any possible way to fix things.

"James, I need you to listen to me, we don't have any time. I want you to find my mum and bring her to Torpor. Her name is Monica Miller, she's just like me, red hair and brown eyes. Promise you won't forget about her." James didn't know what to say, if he agreed with Stevie's request he'd be facing the fact that she wouldn't be able to find her mum with him but a drudge had already started to escort the recruits who hadn't made the cut into the headquarters, so there was no time to protest. "Promise me James," Stevie pleaded, not moving until he agreed.

"I promise, but Stevie I'm going to talk to Vask. There must be some other way," James repeated, refusing to lose eye contact with her until the door was shut behind them.

13. "WE ARE THE ULTIMATE POWER HERE."

That night, James was free to sleep wherever he wanted in Torpor for the first time since he signed up to be a recruit, but even surprising himself, he craved nothing other than his familiar bunk bed in the training dormitory. James thought of going to Liza's, or even to see Anne, but leaving the headquarters didn't appeal to him while Stevie was still stuck there. Some of the other new Whiteflyers seemed to have a similar desire to stay in the bed they'd been using for the last couple of months, or maybe they were just too tired to find alternative sleeping arrangements, and it wasn't long before the excited chatter in the once packed room was replaced by mumbled snores.

James had closed his heavy eyes for what felt like only seconds before he was abruptly awoken by loud banging and a bright light. In a blur of confusion, he quickly sprang out of bed, ready for whatever was coming to get him. "Calm down Moore, it's only us," laughed a familiar voice from near the door. His eyes took a few more seconds to register that it was Watson, and a few seconds again to recognise the people he'd come with, Charlie, Alton, Alice, Elizabeth, Joseph and a few other Whiteflyers that James had seen around the headquarters, but who had never trained him. Matthew and Tim, who were the only new Whiteflyers not to sleep in the recruits room, also stood with them, looking more smug than ever. .

"Well why are you all just standing there, staring at us?" Elizabeth asked when nobody moved. "Get dressed. We're going out." James did as he was told and got dressed into his new whites, not because he wanted to spend any time with the people that Matthew and Tim seemed to already have bonded with, but because he needed to stay on their good side, for the time being anyway. Admittedly a part of him was also curious as to what 'going out' involved in Torpor, where the hospitality, or any industry for that matter, didn't exist and where alcohol was non-existent.

"So, where do you think they're taking us?" Annabelle wondered out loud as they stepped out into the night.

"I don't know, but I heard Charlie say something about an initiation to Alton, so I guess they take all the new Whiteflyers there," James replied mid yawn.

"Maybe it's Arcadius?" Annabelle suggested, excitement filling her face at the thought. "Or maybe Tartarus if they're trying to freak us out." While Arcadius and Tartarus had fuelled James' imagination as possible options, he quickly passed them off as wishful thinking. They'd been told shortly after the challenge that their first introduction with The Controller, and their first journey to another world, wouldn't happen until the following evening and it wasn't likely the Whiteflyers would disobey Hatt so openly.

Close to an hour after leaving the headquarters, the Whiteflyers drew to a halt next to some of the tallest buildings in London. "Why have we stopped?" Matthew asked. "All of these buildings are just filled with cowards and losers. I went into them unknowingly when I first got to Torpor."

"Well then it's a good thing we're not going to go into them," Charlie answered, not even finishing his sentence before he had begun rising into the air, drifting towards one of the medium sized buildings. With a laugh, the others joined him and not before long, the recruits had also sprung into the air, taking full advantage of their powers for the first time.

As he sprang faster and higher through the dark night sky, James could feel the air ruffle his robes and push back his hair. Up here, all of his worries and guilt seemed eons away. On Earth, he didn't venture into the business areas of London much, but when he did, he was always amazed at the sheer size of the buildings. He'd seen even higher ones in New York on TV, and it was one of the many places on his bucket list that he assumed he now would never get the opportunity to explore. However, looking out into the empty air, as he landed on top of a tall crane, he realised that nothing was impossible. If London translated to Torpor, New York must have too, and so must have Italy and Australia and all of the other countries he'd always wanted to visit. High on this idea, James joined everyone as they gleefully jumped from building to building and he even helped Joseph to create a sky bridge between two of the closer skyscrapers. As the buildings they jumped to grew in size, some of the novice Whiteflyers began to slow down. However, encouragement from the others and their own ego, always pushed them to go just that little bit higher, and before anyone realised, they were jumping to the top of the tallest building in the UK, The Shard.

"Cool, that's a helicopter," Tim exclaimed the obvious, as the Whiteflyers landed atop the skyscraper.

"Yes, my friend, it certainly is. And a big one at that," Alton shouted over the loud noise of the propellers, slapping Tim on the back and running towards it. "Everyone jump in."

Elated, the group of recruits lined up and climbed into the beast. James had never even considered helicopters would be in Torpor. Cars were barely ever used, and he certainly had never been in one on Earth. "Where are we going?" he asked Alice, his thoughts running wild with the countries he'd been fantasising about not long before.

"We're Whiteflyers, we don't need to be going somewhere to use a helicopter. Just sit back and take it in. You've never seen London like this before." James did as he was told, and relaxed. Alice was right, this was London from a whole new perspective. The views were spectacular.

After circling the city, the headquarters came into sight and James figured that their journey was coming to an end. He was only just realising how tired he was and was relieved to be getting dropped all the way back to bed. "Well that was a night to remember," Annabelle yawned, stretching out her arms and pulling herself away from the window she'd been glued to since they had taken off.

Elizabeth smiled, a mischievous twinkle in her eye, "And it's only going to get more unforgettable." "Yesterday you were all chosen to become Whiteflyers," Elizabeth explained to the ten fresh faces. "However, tonight is the real test. It will determine whether, or not, WE allow you to become one of us. But don't worry, all you have to do is...jump." As Elizabeth said the last word, she opened the helicopter door and fell backwards, landing in a park not too far from the headquarters. They were nearly 400 ft high, but James wasn't impressed. While jumping would have seemed crazy to him only a few weeks ago, with everything he had learnt since then it wasn't very brave at all.

"Easy!" Tim snorted. "I'll go first."

Charlie grinned from ear to ear at his response, "I'd hold on a second before you do. Elizabeth forgot to mention a crucial part of the jump. Watson, care to share?"

"Yeah, that really was the most important part. Powers are off limits. For as long as your nerves can handle it anyway," Watson explained, just as smugly.

"What do you mean powers are off limits? Why would anyone do that?" Tim asked, his face pale white at the thought.

"Now, now Tim, we aren't totally evil. You can use your powers after you reach a certain height, but we will let you guess what that threshold is on your way down. Anybody who uses them too quickly is out. Cowards don't belong here," Charlie replied.

James felt like an idiot, he should have known it wouldn't have been as easy as building jumping. The Whiteflyers weren't the kind of people to let anyone into their group so easily. Even Watson, who James had always half liked, seemed totally elated at the idea of them jumping out of the helicopter. *How much power did they really have though?* James thought to himself. *Surely, not more than Hatt, Vask and Catherine.* However, realising that they could make his life a lot harder if they wanted to, regardless of whether they could stop him from becoming a Whiteflyer, James decided the best thing was to do it and get it over with fast. "I'll go first," James said, a false confidence oozing out of his voice.

"Of course you will," Joseph affirmed proudly. "You are level four after all." That last sentence annoyed Matthew and he stepped forward almost immediately after to volunteer to go second. Then

Annabelle, then Tessa, and so on until everyone was on board, terrified or not.

As his feet dangled from the open doored helicopter, James' fear left his body. He couldn't die, and that was all that mattered in the end. If this is what it took to bring Liza and Stevie's mum back to Torpor, then this was a small price to pay in comparison to what Stevie would have to endure until he could convince Vask that they made the wrong choice by not picking her to be a Whiteflyer. Closing his eyes and deciding to enjoy it, James tilted his weight over the side of the door, and he let himself fall. His whole body went into a state where he felt as if his blood was-pure adrenaline. If he felt free before, it didn't even compare to this. Picking up speed, he felt like a rocket for a few brief moments before his reality set in and he could see the ground only a dozen or so short meters below him. Activating his power source, he tried to slow his inevitable crash as much as he could. He'd started too late, so a soft landing was out of the question, but at this rate anything short of exploding on the hard pathway would suffice. *Can people even heal if their body parts don't die together?* he wondered as he readied himself for impact, shielding his face with his arms. But seconds later, the impact never came and when he opened his eyes, he was floating a meter above the ground.

"Are you insane?" Elizabeth roared, her face red with an anger James had never seen her show before. "You are allowed to use your powers towards the end. Did someone forget to mention that up there? Should I be bracing myself for the next maniac?"

James blinked, confused about what had just happened. "Eh sorry. I was in the moment. I forgot," he answered, dumbfounded that he was still talking and walking, but relieved that they weren't actually planning to let them turn into human soup. "So how did you stop me anyway?" James asked, when he'd come up to standing as they waited for Matthew to take the leap.

"It's like a heavy air pocket," Elizabeth illustrated, motioning to the empty space he had just landed in. "I started it about 10 metres up. We do expect you to slow yourself down somewhat before though. I wasn't sure if it would stop you before you hit the ground," she added dramatically, still irritated that she was close to being covered in James' inner body parts.

As the rest of the new Whiteflyers jumped from the helicopter, a mix of fear, exhilaration and adrenaline filling their faces, Elizabeth's concerns that she'd have a repeat of James' jump were alleviated. It wasn't, however, until they were all safely back to the ground that Alice, who had been monitoring the point everyone turned to their powers during the impromptu jump, announced the results. "Well it's safe to say James didn't use his powers too early," she laughed. "The rest of you all fell into the normal bracket of 80 to 120 feet above the ground. Well, that's all except Tim, you only managed falling 50 feet before relying on yours." James snorted with laughter louder than he meant to and Watson and Elizabeth joined in. It had always been obvious to James that Tim was a coward, it was one of the reasons he was such a bully, but he was happy to know the knowledge had been received loud and clear by the rest of them.

Tim went bright red and clenched his fist but didn't move towards James. "I jumped off differently to everyone else. I was spinning," he tried to justify.

"Okay Tim, if you say so," Watson replied sarcastically, displaying a toothy grin. "Luckily for you though your only requirement was to jump, so you are all officially Whiteflyers."

As they strolled back to the headquarters, James felt a lot calmer and happier than he had on the way out. While Stevie's position still concerned him, he'd seen a different more friendly part of the other

Whiteflyers that he hadn't seen, or thought was possible before. While he was sure he'd never be friends with the likes of Alton and Charlie, and definitely not Matthew, Tim, Rufus and Rowe, the rest had potential. "So, becoming a level four Whiteflyer wasn't enough was it? You had to show us all up as more cowardly than you too," Annabelle said, humour filling her tone.

"Ah you know me Annabelle, limelight is my middle name," James joked back, nudging her gently.

"I wish Marcus and Stevie were here, but it's not all bad, we still have each other," she replied more seriously. While James was sure Annabelle could never replace the relationship he had with Stevie, they'd always got on, so she wasn't completely wrong. Just as he opened his mouth to voice his agreement, noise coming from just up ahead dragged his attention away.

"What's going on here?" Watson, who had caught up to Charlie and Tim before James did, enquired.

"We were just explaining to these love birds we came across that they shouldn't be out so late. It could be dangerous," Tim answered, gesturing to the two people in front of him, an evil grin highlighting the irony in his voice.

"Sorry we didn't mean to bother anyone. We are just on our way inside. It was just such a lovely night and I am new here. My David did tell me it wasn't safe, but I insisted," an older woman explained, her voice shaking. The man beside her looked nearly twenty years younger, but the words 'lovebirds' did seem to be the correct way to describe them, nonetheless. James figured they must have been together on Earth and died at different times.

"You're not going anywhere," Charlie stated, moving a step to the right to block their path. "How would it look to the other residents if we let just you two do as you please, and right outside our headquarters to boot? Before we knew it, everyone would think they could get away with anything."

The man on the receiving end slowly moved his body to block his wife. "As she explained, she hasn't been here long enough to understand how things work. We don't mean any disrespect. If you could just…" Before James could hear the end of the sentence, Alton had stepped forward and covered his hands in flames.

"There are no deals here," he shouted, louder than was necessary. "We are the ultimate power." The man stepped back in shock, stumbling over the woman and knocking them both to the ground. Watching them lying together on the footpath, with a threatening Alton towering over them, forced James to jump into protective mode and he instantly forced the air to pull Alton back. The sudden loss of his control caught Alton by surprise and he nearly set Alice, who had been standing nearby, on fire.

"Stand down Alton," James demanded. "They said they'll leave. I see no further reason to keep them here." As all of the Whiteflyer's attention turned towards him, the couple intuitively snuck away, but the matter didn't end there as far as anyone, but James, was concerned.

"Are you threatening me Moore?" Alton asked, his face inches from James. "You've been a Whiteflyer for less than a day. I don't take orders from you, or from anyone for that matter."

James didn't reply but embraced himself for what was coming as Alton's flames grew as quickly as his anger. Some of the other Whiteflyers had also joined in and formed a circle around them both, leaving no room for either of them to leave. A few shouted abuse at James from the side lines and cheered Alton on. Even Watson made his alliance clear. "That's not how we run things around here James. Alton shouldn't have reacted that way, but we stick together no matter what. We never undermine each other in front of the residents." All of James' illusions about who these people were just moments before had broken to pieces.

Faster than he could think up a plan, James reacted, building a wall ten feet high and two feet thick. Five blows later and Alton had broken it down. However, by this time, James had formulated a plan and he was ready with a fireball as soon as Alton's face came peeking through the broken-down stone. However, something unexpected happened and with a firing passion, Alton swung at James, realising that his powers were no match. James, expecting a battle of elements, stumbled back with the force. He gathered himself together and lunged forward, cracking Alton in the head with his fist.

Furious, Alton wiped the blood from his face with a quick swipe, and roared into the air, "YOU DARE TOUCH ME. I WILL END YOU." By now, James wanted nothing more than to be away from these people, so instead of responding, he did just as Stevie would have wanted him to and lunged into the air, leaving a threatening trail of fire in his wake. As James sped away, he could hear Joseph, whose power status made him the most senior in a way, ordering Alton to let him go.

Not sure of where to go, James aimlessly flew around Torpor watching the city below him. It all looked the exact same as Earth from up high and it was easy to pretend that nothing had changed. Thinking of what his experience would have ended up like if Liza had woken up beside him in Torpor, subconsciously directed him to her house. It was still vacant and the couch he and Stevie had furnished it with was still in the living room. Without thinking into it too much, and still unsure of where the morning would take him, he let himself fall asleep for the second time that night.

14. "PLEASE WELCOME, THE CONTROLLER."

The next morning, James woke up after the sun came up. It was the first morning since before signing up to become a recruit that he didn't have anything pressing to do. His visit to Arcadius to see The Controller was later on that day, but considering the events of the day before, he wasn't even sure that he was still a Whiteflyer. Maybe Watson's words about sticking together were more than just guidelines, maybe it was a rule? James brushed his thoughts away and decided he would deal with it all later, for now, all he craved was to see a familiar face and luckily for him, one lived right next door.

Anne's door was unlocked as usual, but James still felt uncomfortable walking in without making himself known. Stevie usually didn't bother because Anne protested so much when they did, but James still felt too awkward to barge in unannounced. While he liked Anne a lot, he had not become as close to her as Stevie had. All the same, when Anne's excited face came to meet him at the door, he felt instantly at home. "Come in, come in," she squealed. "What have I told you about ringing the doorbell?" James smiled gently, and without even realising what he was doing, he reached out his arms and embraced her in a long, warm and much needed hug.

"So, where is my Stevie?" Anne asked innocently, her eyes searching the street behind him, as James broke away. James was caught off guard, he had assumed Anne was at the challenge the day before because Tracey was, but on second thought, she would never miss a day of going to the hospital to look for her husband.

"Stevie can't leave the Whiteflyer headquarters, not yet anyway. I am working on it," James replied, pulling at his sleeve awkwardly. Anne gave an all too knowing nod and changed the subject before any more explanation was necessary.

For the rest of the morning, Anne did most of the talking. She filled James in on everything he missed while he was at training, which unsurprisingly included a couple of visits from Tracey. James made a mental note to visit her soon too, but he couldn't imagine her turning a blind eye to the Whiteflyer subject like Anne was, so decided to leave it for another day. One that didn't include his first possible encounter with The Controller. Anne also talked about her weekly trips to see the announcements and her daily visits to the hospital. Her surprise at seeing Stevie and James with Hatt the first week after they'd gone missing was evident, but she thankfully didn't touch on it too much.

James stayed at Anne's well into the afternoon, only leaving when he was sure he couldn't give up any more time before heading back to the headquarters and even then he had to use a car to make sure he got back before dark. Vask hadn't given an exact time that they'd be leaving to go to Arcadius at, not that watches even worked in the Three Worlds, but James figured he should leave some wiggle room in case the night before warranted a conversation or two. While facing Alton and Charlie was on the bottom of his to do list, seeing The Controller was on the very top, and he wouldn't let one negate the other.

"You came back," Annabelle gasped joyfully as James walked into the recruits living quarters. "I wasn't sure you would want to after everything."

"Of course I did. I wouldn't miss it. No matter how much Alton and the others probably wish I would," James replied, looking around the room for Matthew, Tim, or anyone else from their posse.

"They're not here," Annabelle confirmed. "They don't sleep here, remember. A few of the others moved out today too. I think it's probably time we all did. Apparently, there are loads of bedrooms upstairs that we can use. Most of the Whiteflyers stay in the headquarters for the first while."

James shrugged, he knew he couldn't stay in the recruit's dormitories forever, but it was the first place Stevie would look if she came to find him, "Yeah, I guess we can explore the place later and find somewhere else to sleep."

The newest Whiteflyers gathered in the domed entrance of the headquarters waiting for Hatt, Vask and Catherine to bring them to Arcadius to present them to The Controller. None of them had an idea of where they were going to be taken, all they knew was that it wasn't possible for regular residents to get there. James imagined it to be somewhere hidden in a faraway mountain, guarded by Whiteflyers more powerful than even Vask. Annabelle had voiced other ideas of a world in the clouds that required Air to get to but considering most Whiteflyers found it unnerving enough to get to the top of the Shard, James wasn't so sure.

"So, everyone made it," Vask exclaimed as he walked down the stairs, Hatt and Catherine not far behind him. He didn't directly look at James as he said this, but all the same, James felt it was an odd fact to point out unless he had heard about the antics of the night before.

"No bets on who ratted me out," James whispered to Annabelle and glared at Matthew. "I'm sure he was only happy to run to Catherine as soon as he got the chance."

Annabelle shrugged, "You don't know that, any of the more advanced Whiteflyers could have told him what happened." While Annabelle was right, her reply only made James miss Stevie more than he already did. They had never needed a valid reason to complain about Matthew to each other and it wasn't as fun if the person he was venting to didn't share a similar hatred for his enemies.

"Before we get started," Vask proclaimed. "I have something very important to say. While Whiteflyers are free to travel between the Three Worlds, this is not something we do lightly. We belong to Torpor, not Arcadius or Tartarus. Free travel is not permitted without permission from Hatt, Catherine or Myself." James' face dropped; he couldn't believe they were only being told this now. How was he expected to find Liza under the watchful eye of these three dictators?

Before he could help himself, James called out angrily. "We are Whiteflyers now. That wasn't the...", but before he could finish, Vask jumped in, growing redder than James knew possible.

"Don't dare take that tone with me Moore. You may not be a recruit anymore, but you are still under my command. One more outburst like that and you'll regret ever meeting me." Speechless, James nodded lightly to show his recognition. He didn't know what he was thinking, crying out like that in front of everyone. He was more than fed up of being told what to do, but there was a time and a place to voice his frustrations. His anger, mixed with shock, had gotten the better of him. He had assumed that once he became a Whiteflyer he would finally be free, but it turned out he was just swapping one form of authority with another.

Ready for a long journey into the unknown, James was shocked when Catherine, who had been leading the way to the path to Arcadius, stopped shortly after they'd left the headquarters... "Is this it?" Rowe asked, looking mildly unimpressed up at Big Ben's clock tower. "Surely anyone can come here. It's not even guarded."

Catherine rolled her eyes, clearly fed up with having to endure the same reaction from every newcomer. "Yes, but not just anyone can do this," she announced, rising up into the air. When Hatt and Vask followed suit, the rest took their cue and trailed behind. "And not anyone can do this," she stated again, this time moving the small hand of Big Ben to join the big hand at 12. It was the first time James had seen a clock's hands move since coming to Torpor and he wondered if it had anything to do with the lack of time. He supposed the entrances would be made obvious if they were the only clocks not working, but on the other hand, maybe they were chosen as the entrances because they had no other use.

As James thought about this, Big Ben's hands found their target. The face opened and Catherine floated inside, closing it behind her. Half expecting something more to occur, James and some of the others moved a few feet back. However, all that happened was that the hands moved back to their regular holding place of three o'clock. Following suit, Hatt moved forward and did everything exactly as Catherine had, but when the face of the clock opened for him Catherine was no longer inside. He didn't seem at all surprised, he just stepped inside and once again, the door shut behind him. Before anyone had the chance to ask, Vask turned to the newest Whiteflyers to explain, "Clocks dotted around Torpor, Arcadius and Tartarus provide passage between the Three Worlds. This area of Torpor's closest entrance to both Arcadius and Tartarus is at Big Ben. As the brightest among you may have realised, the numbers on the clock denote different destinations. These numbers don't change from world to world. Twelve o'clock will take you to Arcadius, three will bring you here, to Torpor, and six o'clock, to Tartarus. Once the door closes and you reopen it, you will have arrived at your destination."

One by one everyone lined up to finally enter Arcadius. Travelling between the worlds had taken up a healthy portion of the new Whiteflyer's common room talk over the last couple of months, and it was hard to believe that they were finally here. It was bittersweet for James because Stevie wasn't getting to experience it with him, but the image of Liza standing on the other side of the door pushed his irritation aside. Vask was waiting to make sure that everyone made it through, and James was the second last person to turn the hands of Big Ben and travel on to Arcadius. As the door closed behind him, he felt a sudden pang of helplessness. However, it was soon relieved when he spotted a handle attached to the inside of the clock's face. Opening the door, James held his breath, preparing for the worst.

At first glance, Arcadius looked a lot like London to James. Not like Torpor's London, but Earth's. However, by the time he landed on solid ground, his first impression had taken a complete U turn. Like Torpor, the buildings and empty spaces in Arcadius were all modelled on the city he was born in, but in contrast, while Torpor felt dull and lifeless, Arcadius was beaming and full of beauty. Everything somehow managed to sparkle. The meticulously clean red brick walls and large stone buildings were highlighted by a bright red sunset, the likes of which is usually only found on postcards and calendars. The people passing didn't walk aimlessly by, they had a spring in their step and a smile on their face, they walked with a purpose. And perhaps the most different of all were the sounds that filled the streets. A constant flow of chattering and laughter passed through James' ears and at one point, he even heard a dog bark, an impossibility on

Torpor that he didn't even dare dream to find on Arcadius before now.

"Welcome to Arcadius," Hatt announced, as the last person came to solid ground, spreading his arms out for a full effect. "Yes Tim, that is someone eating an ice-cream. Food is widespread in this world," he added, noticing Tim goggling at a man with a coned creamy whip. "While only some of you got the odd treat during your training, you should all be aware that food is allowed in Torpor, might I add solely on headquarter grounds. Nonetheless, because it's brought in from Arcadius, we only eat it occasionally. Either way, you won't see it as much of a novelty next time you visit."

Fully expecting The Controller to live in the Whiteflyers Headquarters in Arcadius, James and three or four of the others started towards Trafalgar Square when Hatt made motions to make a move on, but more surprising than it should have been, Hatt instead made his way towards the Palace of Westminster. "You didn't expect him to live with the likes of you did you," Rowe snorted, following Hatt closely to make sure she made a good first impression on her new master. James followed loosely behind too, but was preoccupied with familiarising himself with Arcadius, and more importantly, looking out for Liza. While it wasn't likely he would bump into her walking down the street, it also wasn't completely impossible, especially if she made the connection about travelling between the worlds and became a Whiteflyer like he did. The headquarters wasn't far away, and for all he knew they hung around in The Controller's palace some of the time. They may even all be meeting him for the first time together. At this last thought, the butterflies in James' stomach went crazy. He hadn't put the two together before, but it was likely that the new Tartarus, Arcadius and Torpor Whiteflyers could all be there. If Liza was made a Whiteflyer in any world he could be seeing her for the first time in months. For the first time since they had died.

On arrival into the Controller's palace, dozens of drudges lined the vast entrance hall, longer and even wider than most rooms. James remembered visiting the Palace of Westminster with his school as a kid, but the grandeur and the splendour here had been magnified tenfold. Gold details covered the floors and ceiling and art that was too precious to be priced lined the walls from top to bottom. Three Whiteflyers stood in the centre of the room, welcoming them. Their similarities with Vask, Hatt and Catherine were uncanny. While they didn't look alike, their demeanour and way of behaving was identical. "Welcome, welcome," the leader of the three, a tall and beautiful but deadly looking woman, announced. "I trust you got to our beautiful world alright."

Hatt, who didn't look at all impressed by this, replied back in jest with a subtle undertone of sarcasm, "Madera, I've been coming here long before you were born. Trust me, I can find my way without getting lost."

Madera laughed louder than was necessary and added, "Oh William, always the joker." James hadn't heard anyone call Hatt by his first name directly before and judging by Hatt's face, he now understood why.

After the Whiteflyer veterans were satisfied with their meagre introductions, the new recruits followed them through the palace and into a lavish dining room, complete with the longest table James had ever seen. And even though the table was extravagantly set with more plates and cutlery than James could possibly see a use for, and the flower arrangements that filled the middle of the table would surely make making eye contact with the people sitting opposite difficult, what caught James attention in full were the ten people, dressed in all white, near the far end of the table. "They must be Arcadius' newest Whiteflyers," Annabelle whispered beside him. Quickly moving his eyes over each person in the room, James' stomach jolted at the sight of someone with long black curly hair sitting near the end of the table, but within a second, he could tell that it wasn't Liza. This woman was at least ten years older, and not nearly as beautiful.

Disappointed, James sat down beside Annabelle at the far end of the table. Unsurprisingly, Rowe, Matthew, and Tim sat as close to the Arcadius Whiteflyers as possible. No doubt trying their best to climb the social ladder early on. While power levels seemed to be the key to respect in these crowds, politics always found a way of making an impact. "Can you believe this place?" Annabelle asked nobody in particular. "I thought our headquarters were nice. I've never been anywhere even close to this fancy before."

Dennis, who kept to himself a lot nodded eagerly, "I know, and it looks as though they're going to feed us too. I wasn't in the winning group that time they gave out popcorn and I've been dreaming about food ever since." Before James had a chance to weigh in on the conversation, the room's attention was brought back to the door, as thirteen new Whiteflyers piled into the dining hall. James' heart sunk as his last hope of Liza becoming a Whiteflyer evaporated. She wasn't standing with the newcomers, which meant she was still lost somewhere.

"They must be from Tartarus," Annabelle stated. "They don't look as I expected though. They don't seem evil."

Irritated, James whipped his head towards her, "They're not evil. Haven't you been paying attention at all? I don't know who you knew on earth, but one in three of my friends certainly don't deserve to end up there." Taken aback by James's snappy response, Annabelle didn't respond and instead turned away to continue her conversation with Dennis.

As the last guests took their seat, the woman who Hatt had greeted as Madera stood up, "Welcome everyone. It's not very often that the Three Worlds, Arcadius, Torpor, and Tartarus, come together for such a joyous occasion as this. For the most part, our dealings are political and not social. However, bringing the newest members of our family together, and I don't say family flippantly, is always an occasion I look forward to." As Madera continued, James scanned the room and realised that there was only one empty seat left, and he immediately caught his breath. They were finally going to meet The Controller. "We will all have time to introduce ourselves and get to know each other shortly, but before that, it's my pleasure to present the man who made it possible for us all to be here today. And when I say here, I don't just mean at this dinner table, but in this magnificent world that I have come to call home. Please welcome, The Controller."

As Madera finished her last two words, the double doors at the top of the room, nearest the empty chair, opened. James held himself steady, fighting the urge to stand up and get a better look. He'd been waiting for this moment from his first day in Torpor. A man, who looked much younger than James had envisioned, walked into the room. His body couldn't have been older than 21, which meant that The Controller would have created the three new worlds when he was only a few years older than James was now. The man looked a lot less intimidating than James and Stevie had painted him in their late night talks. His small stature, sandy blonde hair and pale blue eyes gave him a much softer look than was expected from someone who was responsible for so much pain and unrest.

Before The Controller addressed anyone, he carefully looked around the room, taking a mental note of every person around the long table. When his eyes caught James', James could have sworn the young man spent double the amount of time sizing him up than he had anyone else, but he shook it off as paranoia. After all, James hadn't even introduced himself. When he had made his way through everyone, The Controller greeted his guests, in a deep voice usually found only associated with older characters, "Welcome, welcome. Please don't stay standing on my account." With a smooth motion The Controller pulled his chair out from under the table without touching it and took a seat, prompting the others to do the same. "It is always a great pleasure to meet my newest Whiteflyers for the first time. Although I haven't been physically present at your training, I have been paying close attention to each of you and to your progress from afar. I take a great interest in those who will be working for me. Not everyone deserves the powers I bestow on them and in the early days in particular, I make sure to personally monitor patterns of behaviour. It's not often, but I have found in the past that some people become Whiteflyers for personal gain and not because it is in the best interest of the Three Worlds." At that, the more advanced Whiteflyers nodded and some of the novices looked uneasy. James felt particularly disturbed at the thought of The Controller watching him on his hunt for Liza and Stevie's mum, but how he was planning to watch them was a mystery unknown. James assumed it was just through hearsay, but who knew what power The Controller had in Arcadius, Torpor and Tartarus. "Now enough of that. Let's eat."

Before James could see the food, he knew it was coming. His nose filled with smells of aromatic spices, pungent cheeses and sweet desserts. A dozen drudges lay out the overflowing plates down the middle of the table and as soon as they got the go ahead from the more experienced Whiteflyers, James and the others dug straight in. The only new Whiteflyers not as enthusiastic about the spread in front of them were Arcadius', who had presumably been treated to similar banquets on occasion. "This is worth becoming a Whiteflyer for alone," Tim gasped between mouthfuls of food. "I've never seen so much grub." James found himself agreeing with Tim for the first time in a while. He'd never forgotten how enjoyable food could be, even if hunger wasn't an issue.

"Do you get this in Torpor?" came a voice next to James. "We don't in Tartarus. Then again we don't really get anything special in Tartarus." James turned, realising the question was being addressed to him. The boy sitting beside him looked to be a similar age to himself. He was a skinny guy with a mop of curly light brown hair that made his head look twice the size. "Oh sorry. I'm Grey. Nice to meet you," the boy said, holding out the hand that wasn't holding a dessert waffle.

"I'm James. Eh, we had popcorn once and I think we have access to some food, but definitely not like this. The regular people on Torpor don't get any," James answered, holding out his hand to meet Grey's.

"The Arcadius Whiteflyers don't seem to know how lucky they are here," Grey replied, nodding towards the other side of the table. "It's a whole different world where I come from."

"Yeah, I heard it's pretty tough there. Is it as bad as they say?" James asked, warming to the boy he'd only just met.

"Well that depends what they say about it. I guess you can decide for yourself now that we can move between worlds and all that," he answered. "I'll show you mine, if you show me yours." James laughed, he liked Grey, he reminded him of his friends back on Earth.

James spent the rest of the meal talking with Grey. Grey had been dead for two years before he decided to become a Whiteflyer. He was from an area not too far from James on Earth, so they had a lot in common. Most of the conversation involved video games and their favourite football teams, but towards the end, when James decided he trusted him enough, their conversation grew a bit more serious. "You wouldn't happen to know anyone in Tartarus by the name of Liza?" he asked as casually as he could. "Pretty. Curly, long, black hair."

Grey stared at James for longer than he'd have liked before answering, "No mate. I am afraid not, but I didn't know everyone who signed up to become a Whiteflyer. We were told you only have a 100 or so every year, we've much more than that. It's hard to get to know everyone." James nodded sharply before swiftly turning the conversation back to football. Grey seemed trustworthy, but he barely knew him at the same time, he couldn't risk arousing suspicion, especially after The Controller's warning at the beginning of the night.

Once everyone had finished eating, and the drudges cleared the tables, Madera stood up to command the attention of the room, "At this point of the evening, I'd ask everyone to go around the table to introduce yourself to each other and to The Controller." As Madera said 'The Controller' she bowed in his direction ever so slightly, whether it was a mandatory sign of respect, or if it was just her natural reaction to the most powerful man in the universe, James didn't know. "I shall begin. I am Madera Hall. I am a level 4 Whiteflyer from Arcadius. I have been here for two hundred years."

The introductions continued in the same way, and while James didn't really care to get to know anyone in the room on a personal level, he did find it useful to know who had what power levels. By the time it came to Grey's turn nobody had yet announced that they were a level 4. "Hey, I am Grey Adams. I am a level 3 Whiteflyer from Tartarus and I have been there for two years."

Next James stood and looked around the room. He could swear he saw Hatt's lips turn up into a meagre smile before returning to the neutral expression he momentarily misplaced. "Hey, I am James Moore. I'm a level 4 Whiteflyer from Torpor. I have been there for just a couple of months." At that the room's silence broke and all around him people whispered and stared, uncaring if he could see them.

"Yes, yes. James is the only level 4 Whiteflyer this year. Let's not make him uncomfortable. We still have a few people to get through," Madera said, motioning for everyone to be quiet and for the next person to stand up.

As he sat down, James' eyes caught with The Controller's, and for the first time since meeting him, he sensed danger. There was nothing curious about his stare, it was wholeheartedly threatening. While others were looking at him, The Controller was looking through him. He'd never felt so vulnerable. Shaking it off and breaking eye contact, James feigned interest in Annabelle's introduction, but from the corner of his eye, James could sense that the The Controller didn't feel the need to offer the same pretence.

On their way back to Torpor, the Whiteflyers buzzed with excitement. They'd successfully had their first other worldly trip and met The Controller himself. All of them seemed to be in agreement that he was a lot less intimidating than they had expected, but James knew differently. The most dangerous people were not those who offered a strong exterior but those who were deceivingly deadly. "Well what did you think? Grey seemed cool," Annabelle asked, presumably deciding to forgive James' snappiness from earlier on.

"Yeah, he was," James agreed. "To think he ended up in Tartarus, but we are stuck with Matthew and Tim."

Annabelle shrugged, "Maybe there's more to him than meets the eye."

That night, all James wanted to do was to go to Stevie and tell her everything that had occurred at dinner. He needed to dissect what happened with The Controller with someone who wouldn't just brush it off as paranoia. He didn't understand why he had been so hostile towards him. Surely the more powerful he was the better? He was working for him after all. Stevie would know the answers, she always did. James lifted the covers, debating whether to follow the temptation to find her. She had to be close, he was nearly sure the drudges slept somewhere in the headquarters. But realising that the only person he'd get into trouble was her, he turned over and closed his eyes, attempting to pull himself away from Torpor, if only in his dreams.

15. "TESSA NEVER CAME BACK."

Days had passed since James visited Arcadius and he still hadn't seen Stevie, or any of the other newly appointed drudges, around the headquarters. By now he had moved into one of the more modern vacant rooms in the building with Annabelle and Dennis. Annabelle had been trying to convince him to move for days before but knowing that Stevie could find him if she really needed to had slowed the process. However, when Elizabeth found them still sleeping on their old bunk beds, she had insisted they move to a room more fitting for a Whiteflyer and James couldn't think of any reasonable excuse to stay that didn't include his best friend.

James' new Whiteflyer duties hadn't been too taxing, mostly involving sporadic patrols of the areas in the North of the city, so he had a lot of spare time leftover to explore the old National Art Gallery. Even still, he hadn't managed to visit every room yet. He couldn't imagine the building was this large on Earth, but then again any of the level 4 Whiteflyers could have manipulated it to grow an extra room, or even a whole other floor if they wanted to. James imagined over the years it gradually expanded, to eventually become what it is today. Only the night before, James came across a room in one of the basement floors that looked like it hadn't been occupied in over a hundred years. Dust covered the stacks of books and hung up paintings, and white sheets were hastily thrown over random bits of furniture. It looked like the attic of an old woman who spent her life hoarding whatever antiques she could get her hands on. James imagined his younger self spending hours rummaging through the drawers and climbing into the nooks and crannies of every corner searching for treasure with Liza.

"Do you want to come on a fly tonight? Some of the others are going to have some fun at the Tower of London. Apparently, some old Earthly royals spend their days aimlessly walking the grounds. It's like it's really haunted," Annabelle asked, as she lounged on her bed throwing a stone into the air.

"Yeah, with Alton and the rest. I think I'll pass," James answered, more bluntly than he should have. It wasn't Annabelle's fault that he didn't get along with them after all.

"You can't avoid them forever, eventually you will have to learn to be around them. You're missing out on all the fun," Annabelle groaned, annoyed that James refused to do anything that involved Alton, Charlie, Tim or Matthew since the night they went building jumping.

"Watch me," James retorted, before exiting their bedroom. While he didn't mention it to Annabelle, Alton wasn't the only reason he declined the offer to visit the Tower of London, he had other plans that night.

"Come in," came the voice from the other side of the door. James held his breath and turned down the door handle to Vask's office. He had been putting off confronting his old trainer for as long as possible, but his futile efforts in finding Stevie made the meeting inevitable. "Moore, I wasn't expecting to see you," Vask said skeptically. "It's not often that novice Whiteflyers come knocking on my door without being called on."

James hesitated, but then thought of his promise to Stevie and stepped inside, "I had a question about the challenge last week. Do you have a spare moment?"

Vask studied James before nodding, "Very well, but make it quick." Hurrying to gather his thoughts together in his head, James moved towards Vask to bide some time, "I was wondering... Well, I wanted to know why Stevie Miller wasn't chosen to be a Whiteflyer? I've watched everyone that was picked in training and some didn't deserve it as much as she did." Vask didn't look as surprised as James imagined he would have, if anything he looked as if he had been expecting this.

"James, I'm not in the habit of explaining my, and my fellow Whiteflyer's decisions to inexperienced newcomers. If Stevie wasn't picked, it was because people better suited to the job were. I will tell you though, as I have been watching you these last few days and I have noticed it is causing you a fair bit of distress, that it was a close call and certain factors unrelated to her performance came into play." Unsatisfied, James went to argue his point but was cut short before the words left his mouth. "That will be all James. Close the door behind you." Positive it would do more harm than good to disagree, James reluctantly obeyed.

For the next two weeks, James tried his best to interact with the Whiteflyers more. He realised that distancing himself from everyone was only punishing himself. He needed human interaction if he was going to stay sane, and he needed to stay sane if he was going to complete his goals. He figured once he didn't directly socialise with Alton, Charlie, Matthew or Tim, it was okay to join their sporadic adventures around Torpor. In addition, Vask's warning of him being watched the night he went to his office, reminded him a lot of The Controller's threat and he thought it was best to join everyone if he wanted to avoid standing out.

Recently, James had also tried, multiple times, to be granted access to Tartarus and Arcadius to find Liza, but his requests were always denied. However, Hatt had recently declared that the level 3 and level 4 Whiteflyers were all invited to The Controllers palace after the public announcement that Sunday, so James didn't have long to wait for another chance at finding out more about Liza. He hadn't asked him to, but he hoped Grey might have taken the initiative to ask around about her and maybe he could even talk to one of the Arcadius Whiteflyers about whether or not Liza signed up as a recruit there.

"So why do you think The Controller wants to see us?" Annabelle asked, as they made their way to Big Ben to meet the rest of the Whiteflyers going to Arcadius.

"I'm not sure, but the others are pretty annoyed the invitation wasn't extended to them. Watson said it wasn't unusual for him to only invite certain Whiteflyers though. I'm just happy to get another look at Arcadius, I feel we didn't get to properly take it in last time."
Annabelle smiled widely in excitement at the thought of getting to go again, "Yeah I did think we'd have more freedom to explore the other worlds. I didn't realise it would only be for scheduled visits. But then again, I suppose everyone would just spend all of their time in Arcadius if it wasn't monitored."

James' second time using the clock's head to visit another world was a lot less fun than the first. This was partially down to the novelty and surprise wearing off and partially down to the longer queue. Arcadius on the other hand, didn't lose any of its spark. If possible, it was even better than he remembered. On arrival to the other world, a waft of freshly baked buns hit his nostrils, as a child walked by with half a dozen cupcakes, instantly getting his visit off to a great start. As he walked to the palace, James couldn't help but gaze at the hundreds of flowers that lined the red brick building's windows and pathways. The evening sun had not done them justice the first time around. The same was true for the immaculate carved statues of lions, birds and men that sat atop the rooftops watching over the people of Arcadius. "It never gets old," came Joseph's voice from behind him.

"Am I being that obvious? I never thought I would be the kind to care for flowers," James laughed.

Joseph snorted, "They're not just your regular flowers though, are they? And they're certainly not your regular buildings. It's not just around where The Controller lives either, everywhere in Arcadius is like this. You should see the countryside. I've never seen anything like it."

Tessa, who was walking nearby, jumped in at that, "Do we get to see that? I'd love to be able to explore."

Joseph laughed to himself, "Sure you get to. You just need to build up some trust first is all."

Unlike James' first visit to the palace, Madera didn't come to meet The Controller's visitors from Torpor on arrival. Instead, a cross looking drudge led them to a large room already occupied with the level 3 and 4 Whiteflyers from the other worlds. As soon as they entered, Grey came running up to James to say hello, "I've saved you a seat. It looks like there is going to be some sort of display or announcement. The Controller isn't here yet though. Have you heard anything?" James grinned and shook his head before walking over to his seat. He was finding it enjoyable getting to know Grey now that he couldn't see Stevie. It felt like he had a friend again.

"No, we haven't been kept in the loop at all."

When everyone had taken their seats and the room had quietened down, Hatt, Madera, and an old bearded man that James recognised from their dinner as Tartarus' head Whiteflyer, Amos, stood up. But instead of addressing the room as expected, they stood to the side, waiting for something, or more accurately someone, to join them. "Isn't it funny to see them so vulnerable? Amos always comes across so high and mighty to everyone, and look at him now, he is just as scared as the rest of us to step out of line in front of The Controller," Grey whispered into James' ear. Shocked that someone other than Stevie was ballsy enough to criticise the system, and in a room full of Whiteflyers, James didn't know how to react. Fortunately, the arrival of The Controller just then relieved him of the need for a response, however, it did leave James with more than one unanswered question.

"It's always a great day when the most powerful people in the universe gather together," The Controller began. "While it would have been great if we could include every Whiteflyer in today's meeting, the numbers don't always make it possible." James couldn't help but shake his head. The Controller had created the Three Worlds from nothing, he was sure he could expand the hall to make room for everyone. He figured the real reason for the exclusion had more to do with a show of superiority than logistics. "As most of you will know, unless you have just newly joined us, the last number of years have seen an increasing number of people from Earth. As their population expands, so does ours. The cities around Arcadius, Torpor and Tartarus are becoming too overcrowded to cater to everyone. To combat this in the past, we have maneuvered the population from cities in the East of the worlds into the countryside. The time has come to employ this tactic across the main cities in the west of the worlds."

Not sure if he was understanding it correctly, James turned to Annabelle to clarify. "Is he saying they're going to relocate people out of London?" Afraid to be heard, Annabelle nodded carefully, a nonchalant expression on her face. "They can't do that. How will their families find them when they die?" James protested.

Once again Anabelle said nothing, so James turned to Grey to direct his horror elsewhere. "Are you really surprised mate? They've no problem splitting us between worlds, what makes you think they care where we live? Grey answered, before James had even voiced his concern.

For the rest of the morning, The Controller was joined by Hatt, Madera and Amos as they explained the processes that they would gradually be putting into place to redirect some of the people outside of the main cities. Not once did anyone mention the consequences for the residents that the move would cause. James couldn't help but think of Anne who was settled in her life. She would be heartbroken if she was one of the ones chosen to move. In total, one third of the people would be moved out of London, and even if James could prevent Anne from being chosen, there were so many more like her roaming the hospitals and their old houses that he wouldn't be able to help.

The next morning, James didn't get out of bed until late. Instead, he spent a lot of time thinking, not only about what The Controller had discussed with them the night before, but about Grey's response to the events that had unfolded. Grey's reaction to the head Whiteflyers and The Controller made James feel like he wasn't the only Whiteflyer who yearned for a better society. He tried to get Grey alone before Hatt ushered them back to Torpor, but it was made impossible by the excitement surrounding the relocation announcement. He also wanted to find out if he had looked into

Liza's whereabouts more, but with no chance to ask, he contented himself with the thought that Grey would have found a way to tell him if he knew anything.

"What are you still doing in bed?" Annabelle asked excitedly, storming into their room. "Haven't you heard?" Curious as to what was going on, James sat up and reached for his robes.

"Let me guess, someone finally built up the courage to set Alton on fire?" he answered sarcastically.

Ignoring James' smart remark Annabelle answered her own question, "Tessa never came back. Apparently, she's in Arcadius now with The Controller. I didn't even notice that she wasn't with us last night, but come to think about it, Matthew was walking back alone."

Taken off guard, James jumped up to get ready faster. "What do you mean she's with The Controller?"

Annabelle shrugged, "I don't really know the details, but Watson said that every now and again he summons a Whiteflyer or two to move in with him. They're always girls, and let's face it, Tessa isn't ugly." James couldn't believe what he was hearing, surely The Controller couldn't just keep Whiteflyers for himself. Knowing Tessa, she would be more than happy to oblige, but it was the principal of it.

James eagerly followed Annabelle through the headquarters to find the others. She was no doubt taking him to the lounge area a lot of them hung around in during their spare time. "Oh, and did I mention, there was one more piece of news?" Annabelle stated joyfully just as she turned into the room. Before James could ask what it was, a familiar redhead made it obvious.

"I'm back!" Stevie exclaimed, running towards him. Unsure of what was happening, James dodged the incoming hug and took a step back. Stevie couldn't be back, it wasn't possible. Vask had made it very clear in training that only ten people would be chosen. Nonetheless, her white robes said differently.

"Back? As a Whiteflyer?" James questioned.

"Yes as a Whiteflyer." She gave a little twirl. "They don't just let anyone wear these..." but before Stevie could finish, James picked her up into a heartfelt hug, which until that moment, he didn't realise how badly he needed.

"You're back," he gasped quietly in disbelief.

"Yes, yes she's back. Now let her down. You're not the only one who missed her," Annabelle demanded. "She wouldn't tell us anything until you got here."

For the rest of the afternoon, Stevie told Annabelle and James about life as a drudge and they in turn told her about their first few weeks as a Whiteflyer. It turned out Vask himself called for her this morning to tell her the news. Because The Controller had hijacked Tessa they were allowed to nominate one more Whiteflyer to take her place, and as Stevie narrowly missed out in the first place, she was the obvious choice. Life as a drudge seemed to be just as James had pictured it. They were all cramped into living quarters behind the headquarters and summoned to do anything the Whiteflyers deemed themselves too important to do. Marcus was taking it better than Stevie had, which James put down to his army background. Richie on the other hand had still not adjusted. "He, and some of the others, spend their nights planning an escape, but it's all empty words really, they wouldn't really dare," Stevie explained, making sure that nobody else was listening in. "I can't believe I made it out. I almost feel bad."

Annabelle instantly shook her head and squeezed Stevie's hand, "Don't be silly. You deserve to be here, you always have."

With the listening ear of Annabelle, James decided against telling Stevie about his first meeting with The Controller, and about Grey, until they were alone. And to his annoyance, he didn't get his moment until the following evening. Under the facade of showing Stevie around the headquarters, he led her to the old abandoned room that he'd found on his first hunt for the drudge's living area. "You really know the way to a girl's heart," Stevie joked as she fingered dust off an ancient cabinet. "What's with all the secrecy? Couldn't we have just left the building?"

James cringed, feeling pretty foolish for not thinking of that first, "Never mind where we are. I've loads to fill you in on.

For the next while, James took Stevie through everything that had happened while she was gone, including what Vask had said about why she wasn't initially picked to become a Whiteflyer. "I've been thinking about that myself", she said, "All of the other recruits have echoed my conviction that my performance was better than some of the people who were picked, and much better than Tim's. I actually think it came down to Catherine. She never liked me, I asked too many questions, and Tim would be her obvious choice. He's Matthew's best friend after all."

James rolled his eyes and shook his head at the injustice, "But you did so well in her history essay? I saw yours; it was so much more detailed than anyone else's."

Stevie shrugged, "Yeah I've been thinking about that too. Maybe the essay isn't really about what you know, but more about the version of history you choose to believe. Thinking back, I added some things I shouldn't have. It was filled with too much opinion. I reckon it set me back, rather than pushing me forward." James supposed that made sense. What did The Controller really care what they knew of their history, once it was in his favour?

"I really don't know why The Controller was acting so weird with you. Are you sure he wasn't just impressed? Or maybe he acts like that with everyone?" Stevie wondered, moving onto the next dilemma.

"No, it was definitely just to me. I wasn't being paranoid, and it was definitely a show of intimidation. There was nothing positive about it," James insisted, annoyed that he was being questioned.

"I believe you, but remember I wasn't there. I'm trying to visualise it for myself," Stevie snapped back, sensing his irritated tone. "I guess I'll just have to suss it out for myself at the next meeting in Arcadius. I can't wait to meet Grey too. He seems like my kind of guy."

Leaving the room to go and find the others before Annabelle grew suspicious, James added, "Yeah he's pretty cool alright. It'd be good to find out why he decided to become a Whiteflyer in the first place though. That way we can decide for ourselves how trustworthy he is."

Over the next week, Stevie and James visited Anne and Tracey to check in on them and assure them that they were doing well. Anne, who had been evidently holding in her worry that Stevie hadn't come with James the first time he visited, shed a tear when she saw her coming up the road. Tracey, who had never met her before, was just happy that James had a friend who he could count on. "Well, I am just relieved that you didn't succumb to the lure of becoming a Whiteflyer for the power. I thought I was hearing things when I came around to check on you and Anne had told me she saw you at the headquarters," Tracey shared, after James shot down the idea that he had become a Whiteflyer for power.

"Of course I didn't. I've got my reasons, and I won't go into them now, but rest assured it has nothing to do with controlling the people of Torpor," James explained, avoiding going into too much detail.

All the same, you need to be careful. You're working very closely with some very dangerous people," Tracey replied, concern showing on her face.

"Don't worry Tracey," Stevie chimed in. "If anything, bad happens, they'll have just as much to worry about as we do. James is a level 4 after all." A crimson James knew this wasn't all that true, he was no match for some of the more experienced Whiteflyers in Torpor, but if it alleviated Tracey's tension, he wasn't going to argue.

Before visiting, Stevie and James decided against telling either of them about the relocation that would be happening over the next few months because Hatt had announced another meeting with The Controller to put the thoughts from the last meeting into actions. Stevie thought it was best she and James find out as much about it as they could before they scared anyone, and they didn't even know if either of them would be relocated anyway. A list of areas was to be revealed in the next meeting in Arcadius.

"I am so excited. Is it as amazing as we imagined it would be?" Stevie asked on the morning of her first visit to see The Controller.

"Yeah it really is. Did I tell you they have animals there?" James replied.

"No, you most certainly did not," she gasped, shocked that he could leave out such a vital piece of information. "I begged my uncle for years to get me a dog, but his lifestyle didn't really allow for it. But my neighbour had the cutest little fluff ball named Bonnie and if she ever went away or needed a babysitter, she let me mind her."

James smiled at the twinkle in her eyes, "Well, as much as I'd love for you to live out your dog mum dreams now, bringing one back isn't really an option. We might not even see any. They don't exactly let us explore when we're there. Well they didn't the last two times anyway. Joseph did say we would get to eventually though, so let's see how it works out."

Stevie's reaction to Arcadius was even better than James had expected. She was generally a very excitable person who couldn't control her emotions very well, so her overwhelmed expressions at her surroundings were something of a delight to those around her. "Have you ever seen that movie where everything is colourful and shiny? The guy with the scissors for hands is in it. That's what this feels like. I'm Edward," Stevie gasped, turning in circles to make sure she didn't miss anything.

"Pretty cool right?" James asked rhetorically.

"Yeah and who knew the entrance was just down the road from the headquarters this whole... Oh and there's a cat," Stevie stated, running across the road to pet the overly hairy black cat. James took a brief glimpse at Catherine, just in time to notice her look at disgust, staring at Stevie picking the animal up.

"I guess Stevie was right, Catherine is not her biggest fan," he thought to himself.

On arrival to the same meeting room as before, James walked straight over to Grey to introduce him to Stevie. "So, I finally get to meet the infamous Grey," Stevie greeted him, ignoring his outstretched hand and going in for a hug.

"This is Stevie. She just got newly assigned Whiteflyer status," James introduced her, realising he hadn't actually told Grey about her yet.

"Ah, even more beautiful than in my dreams," Grey retorted, pretending he'd heard about her before.

"So, you didn't forget about me after all?" Stevie replied, smiling at James. "I thought once I walked out of the stadium that was it for us."

Annabelle chimed in then, "Nope he certainly didn't. He's been moping around the headquarters since you left." James grew bright red and contemplated manipulating the ground beneath his feet to swallow him up.

For the rest of the afternoon, Grey and Stevie got to know each other, as a few dozen drudges circled the rooms handing out canapés and drinks. James hadn't drunk alcohol since before Earth and felt buzzed after only two. It wasn't until everyone had properly relaxed that they were ushered to their seats. Purposely grabbing hold of Grey's shoulder, James not so subtly pulled him back to ask him something he'd been trying to find the time to discuss since he'd got there. "I know I didn't ask you to, but any chance you asked around about Liza, she's the girl I asked you about at our first dinner?"

Grey slowly shook his head, his eyes pitiful, "Sorry mate, I asked a few of the others, but nobody's heard of her. If she is in Tartarus, it looks like she didn't sign up to be a Whiteflyer." Half deflated that he was still no closer to finding her and half happy that she was less likely to be in Tartarus, James took his seat and zoned out as The Controller went into great detail about the relocation.

"James, are you listening to me?" Stevie moaned quietly, snapping him out of his slightly drunk daydream. "I saw you talking to Grey about Liza, has he heard about my mum?" James' head spun, as a pang of guilt rose from his gut. He had briefly thought of asking about her at the dinner, but he just didn't see the point. Tartarus was huge. The only reason he'd asked about Liza was because she'd just died. She was way more likely to become a recruit. Knowing the answer before he said it, Stevie shook her head annoyed, "Of course you didn't. You don't even know where Liza is, I told you I know that my mum is in Tartarus. I would have asked for you." Knowing there was nothing he could say to make it better, James stayed silent and instead gripped her arm with his hand. But with a quick shrug, Stevie made it perfectly clear she didn't want to be touched.

Bringing his attention back to the presentation, where Madera was now going through Arcadius' plans by area, James' eye was immediately drawn to The Controller. He was openly staring at him and Stevie, smiling. Not a happy smile, but one that hid a hint of victory. But the interaction only lasted a heartbeat or two, before the eye contact was broken and James was left with a bad taste in his mouth and a heavy feeling in his chest. Not wanting to give The Controller any more ammunition to associate him with Stevie, James spent the rest of the day ignoring both her and Grey's conversations. Not that Stevie was directing any his way after their disagreement. She didn't even acknowledge him when Hatt disclosed that Arcadius' and Tartarus' newest Whiteflyers would be visiting Torpor over the next couple of days, and that the same visit would be made back to Tartarus the following week.

The next morning, James was abruptly awoken by a visibly upset Annabelle. James immediately jumped up to eye Stevie's bed. The only reason Annabelle would go to him instead of Stevie if she was upset, was if the latter was preoccupied. "Where is she?" he asked in a panic, seeing the vacant and unmade bunk.

"She's gone to Arcadius. Catherine escorted her there earlier, she said that you two weren't speaking and not to bother waking you, and that she'd be back before the end of the day. But Matthew is in the living area now saying she's not coming back. She's been taken just like Tessa has." James sprang out of bed and headed straight for the room he'd been surprised in by Stevie just the week before.

"Where is she?" he shouted, grabbing Matthew tightly by the front of the robe.

"Calm down Moore," came Watson's voice from behind him. "This wasn't Matthew's doing and you know that. The Controller likes to be surrounded by pretty Whiteflyers, he must have just noticed her yesterday and taken a shine to her."

Whipping his head around and loosening his grip, James searched for answers, "But he just took Tessa. You said he only takes a couple of girls every few years? What does he need with Stevie too?" but just as he said it, the answer came to James. The Controller saw them talking the day before, he saw James touch her on the arm. He knew she meant a lot to him. "It's all my fault," James confessed quietly to nobody in particular.

"Yeah it really is," Matthew replied, shoving his hands off his robes. "You don't have much luck with the ladies, do you?"

Before James could react, Watson had grabbed hold of him, anticipating his reaction. "Relax James! She's in Arcadius, and in The Controllers palace no less. How much trouble can she really be in?

I'm sure she will be treated like a queen. She will have everything she has ever wanted."

Back in his room, James let out all of his anger by drilling a hole into the wall, and then another, and another. "How could she not wake me? I would have insisted she stayed," he spouted angrily to a much more cheerful Annabelle.

"Didn't you hear Watson? She's probably better off than us now. She can eat what she wants. She could probably even keep that cat she was playing with if she really wanted to." However, James knew differently, with The Controller's evil grin etched in his brain, he knew exactly why he took Stevie, and it wasn't to give her a better life. It was to get under James' skin. To show him who's more powerful. But why he was so concerned with him, was still a complete mystery.

16. "NOW...WE RUN!"

After the shock of the first day, it seemed from the outside that James was taking the news of Stevie's new place of residence just fine. His outbursts were under control and he painted a happy go lucky smile on his face whenever anyone brought up the subject of her departure. However, the face James masqueraded from the outside was in complete contrast to what was happening on the inside. He didn't see it as a holiday or a change of location, as many of the others had been phrasing it, it was a kidnapping, and there were no other fitting ways to describe it.

James spent his nights planning Stevie's rescue. She was in immediate danger in the hands of The Controller and while James' powers were only a fraction of what the ruler of the Three World's was capable of, he at least had mastered all four levels. Stevie only had access to two and would be useless against Earth or Water if she had to go up against The Controller for any reason. James couldn't sleep picturing her stuck in his palace. She was never one to hold her tongue and follow orders. Unlike Tessa, the thought of being practically owned by someone would destroy her. James didn't have long to wait until he could begin the first phase of his plan to free her, but he needed help, and it wasn't going to come from anyone in Torpor. He needed Grey.

The drudges littered the Whiteflyer's headquarters on the day the newest Tartarus and Arcadius Whiteflyers were coming to visit, trying to get the place ready for their visitors. After a brief tour around the central areas of Torpor's London they would be escorted back to the headquarters for dinner and entertainment. Hatt had demanded everything be kept utterly spotless, no doubt to avoid any unwanted commentary from Madera.

"You seem on edge," Annabelle announced frankly, too loudly and publicly for James' liking.

"Do I? I guess I'm just excited. It's not often we have visitors. It will be good to see Grey again," he replied, trying his best to seem casual.

"Yeah, I suppose it'll be fun, but I'd rather we were going to see what Tartarus is like. Grey's always so vague when I ask him about it," she replied, pulling her hair out of her face. "Then again, I suppose it's not really something to be proud of."

"Do you remember if Hatt announced if we'd be going back to Arcadius too? We haven't really explored there and if they'll be looking around Torpor, it's only fair we get to have a better look around Arcadius," James slyly asked, hoping that the conversation was leading enough to avoid suspicion.

Annabelle glared a while before answering, but it didn't seem that she was sceptical of his intentions, "Yeah I was thinking that too, but no he didn't say." James lifted his eyebrows and nodded, before swiftly changing the subject. That wasn't the answer he was hoping for, but it was the one he had prepared for.

"This isn't all that bad," Grey expressed to James and Annabelle as they flew around the city. "You're in for an awful surprise when you get to my world. Don't get me wrong, Torpor's no Arcadius, but it's probably the closest translation to Earth out of the Three Worlds, so really you should feel right at home."

James shrugged, "Yeah I suppose it's not that bad. It's awfully boring if you're not a Whiteflyer though. The residents do the same thing day in and day out, with as little enthusiasm as possible. Very few still get hopeful or excited. The Whiteflyer's challenge was as lively as I've seen them, and even that buzz didn't last very long."

Grey frowned, looking behind him as they crossed the River Thames, "Speaking of lively. Where's Ms Stevie?"

James went to answer, but Rowe, who was flying close by, beat him to it, her tone filled with bitterness, "For some bizarre reason, The Controller summoned her. She lives in Arcadius now with him and Tessa, and whoever else he deemed worthy enough. It's only a matter of time before he grows bored of her though. Who wants to spend that much time with Miller?"

Grey looked at James, searching for a signal that Rowe's interruption was untrue, but when none came, he turned back to defend his new friend, "Actually, I thought she was extraordinary. Being bubbly, funny and attractive doesn't come around often; not that you'd be familiar with any of those qualities... What was your name again?" Rowe stuck up her chin and let out a loud huff, flying ahead to find Matthew and Tim, no doubt to vent her dislike of James' newest friend.

"So, what's that all about?" Grey asked James and Annabelle once they were out of earshot of Rowe and anyone else that might be considered untrustworthy.

"Yeah, she left the morning after we all visited Arcadius. I'm sure we will see her next time we visit Arcadius though," James replied, conscious that Annabelle was involved in the conversation too. Grey parted his lips to push back on James' carefree attitude but closed them again when his recipient opened his eyes widely.

"Yeah, we thought it was bad too at first, but we've come around to the idea. She's in Arcadius after all, she will have everything she wants. If anything, I am a little jealous. I do miss her though," Annabelle added, unaware of the subliminal messages that were being passed to and fro beside her.

For the rest of the day, James eagerly waited for the opportune moment to talk to Grey in private, but it wasn't until after dinner that a chance presented itself. "Should I show you around the headquarters?" he asked, making sure not to include anyone but Grey in the conversation, but still keeping his tone light in case anyone could overhear.

"Yeah that would be great. Where does the famous James Moore sleep? The first level 4 Whiteflyer in the last 37 years. More if we only count Torpor," he mocked, following James through the crowd and out into the vacant hallway.

"Not here!" James muttered, before Grey could get the chance to ask any of the multiple questions that were probably floating around his head. "I know somewhere we can talk," he added, leading Grey to the abandoned room, he had used once before to avoid any ears in the walls.

"Okay, we are here. Now, can you tell me what's going on? Surely you can't be okay with that man taking Stevie?" Grey asked, outrage filling his voice.

James ran his sweating fingers through his hair, not wanting to confide too much in Grey, but knowing he couldn't rescue Stevie alone all the same, "Why did you become a Whiteflyer?"

Shocked at the question, Grey scrunched up his nose and took a step back, "What's that got to do with anything? We are talking about Stevie here, not me."

James sighed, "Please just trust me. It has everything to do with it. Since I met you, you've acted differently to anyone else that signed up, anyone else but me and Stevie. If I know the reason why you applied, I will know if I can trust you."

Grey stared ahead for a long time before answering, "And how do I know if I can trust you? It goes both ways you know."

Aware that this was coming, James partly answered his own question, making sure to not disclose anything that would get him into too much trouble if Grey was found out to be untrustworthy. "I signed up to find my girlfriend from Earth. I put her in danger and it's my responsibility to get her out of it."

Grey nodded once, confirming that James' answer was suitable enough to reveal his own, "I was sick of Tartarus. None of us belong there. I thought it was time to do something about it."

Relief flooded through James' body; he was right about Grey. "Then let's do something about it. Stevie and I can help you. We all have the same end goal. We've talked about it countless times. But first, we need to set her free."

As quickly as he could, to avoid their absence going noticed in the dining room, James took Grey through the plan he had been formulating in his head since Stevie's disappearance. Agreeing with it for the most part, and improving it in some areas, Grey was completely onboard. Because Stevie's exact location in The Controller's palace was unknown, there were gaps in the plan that would have to rely on improvisation, but they were hopeful that the sheer unthinkability surrounding breaking into the most dangerous residence in all the Three Worlds would give them an advantage. After all, why would anyone put barriers in place to prevent intruders, if they had absolute control over Arcadius, Torpor and Tartarus?

The first stage of James' plan was set to take place in four nights' time, when he would meet Grey in Arcadius by the clock tower, so until then he had to keep his head down and play it safe. He decided it was best if he slept in Liza's over the next few nights to avoid questions before they went into action. He was also keen to spend more time with Anne. He was conscious that he wouldn't be able to see her for some time, and he didn't want to have both he and Stevie ghost her for a second time. He was satisfied that both her and Tracey would be safe in the first round of relocations, as their resident areas weren't being targeted, but he couldn't guarantee that forever. If anything was to happen while he was gone, he wanted to make sure she was in the know and wouldn't be scared.

"It's not the worst of situations, nothing bad will happen to you or to anyone who has to relocate, you just won't get to live in this house anymore. There will be plenty of other places, and they will most likely have bigger gardens and there will be more space for you to relax in," James explained for the fourth time since arriving at his old house.

"Yes, yes, I get that, but nonetheless I'll have to decline if they come around asking me to move. I need to be here when my husband arrives. A big garden is useless if I have to sit in it on my own," Anne refuted.

James took a deep breath, while he was sure Anne's husband would already have arrived at Torpor if it was the world he was destined for, he was anxious not to burst the old woman's hopes by sharing his thought process, "I don't think they will be asking Anne. You know what most Whiteflyers are like. It's important you don't kick up a fuss. As I said, there are no plans to move you yet, and there may never be, but if in the worst case scenario it happens, you will have to go with them. Stevie and I will come and find you. It won't be forever. I promise."

Anne shook her head, unsatisfied with the arrangements, "Why do you and Stevie have to leave at all? If you stayed, you could sort it out for me before anything needed to change. Where is Stevie anyway? It's not like her to not say goodbye."

James raised his eyebrow, trying to think of a believable excuse on the spot, "Of course she would have if she was able to. She was whisked away on Whiteflyer business before she got the chance. She sent me instead. Am I not good enough?" he asked jokingly, eager to lighten the mood.

"Oh of course you are darling. But it would have been nice to see you both off. Anyway, I'll do as you say if it comes to it and I'll let Tracey know the same, just as you've asked." James wiped the sweat off his brow and sighed with relief. Knowing they were both safe and prepared would make a possible temporary exile that much easier if he was caught trying to free Stevie.

James couldn't concentrate on anything except his plans to find and rescue his best friend on the day in question. "Are you sure you want to stay in that house again on your own?" Annabelle asked as the sun went down, and not for the first time since he had told her of his new sleeping arrangements.

"Yeah I'm sure. We spent so much time with all of the other recruits during training, I'm just catching up on some much needed time away from all the craziness. It won't be for much longer," he replied, trying to sound as natural and convincing as possible.

"And you're sure you don't want me to come with you?" Annabelle pushed, not happy that he was spending so much time away from the other Whiteflyers.

"No, you stay here. It would feel weird sleeping there with anyone but Liza," he lied, secretly feeling guilty that he'd spent so much alone time there with Stevie yet dared to use Liza as an excuse. "If you say so. But don't forget about the meeting tomorrow first thing, Hatt will be pissed off if anyone misses it."

As James waved goodbye to Annabelle, he couldn't help but think that it might be for the last time for quite some while. If he was found in The Controller's Palace without reason, who knew what would happen to him. One thing that he was sure of though, was that his powers would be taken away from him and his Whiteflyer status would be stripped. Maybe they'd be satisfied with making him a drudge, but what would happen to Stevie? He had no idea.

James headed in the general direction of Liza's house until he was confident that he was out of sight of any wandering eyes at the Whiteflyer's headquarters. There was still some time left before the sun disappeared completely, but he wanted to arrive at Big Ben early to make sure he was physically and mentally ready to travel to Arcadius without getting caught. When he got there, James circled the area, keeping his eyes peeled for any rogue Whiteflyers that could potentially identify him. Luckily their white outfits didn't make it hard to tell who was just a resident and who was not. When the coast was clear, and he was sure there was nobody risky in sight, he took a deep breath and floated up towards the clock's face.

When James got to Arcadius, he quickly took cover behind one of the many bloom filled bushes and changed into the drudge's outfit he had stolen from the headquarters a few days previous. That was Grey's idea. He had figured that the Whiteflyers in The Controller's palace would easily recognise one another but would see themselves above being familiar with the help. If two strange guys in the Whiteflyer's uniform were seen walking around the palace it would ring alarm bells, but in the drudge's black's, they'd be almost invisible.

James stayed hidden in line of sight of Big Ben, trying to avoid suspicion until Grey appeared. But time went on and he began to grow anxious as to whether Grey was coming at all. Starting to panic, James replayed his conversation with Grey over in his head, wondering whether a miscommunication on the day or time might be the reason for his absence. He tried to push thoughts of betrayal and trust out of his head, blaming everything else before the obvious explanation was the only one left. James didn't know Grey for very long, for all he knew he was working closely with The Controller himself. All of his talk about making a better life for the people of Tartarus meant nothing when James had no actual proof of his intentions. Thinking back to their first meeting, James remembered clearly how eager Grey had been to spark up a conversation. Nobody else at the table seemed to get shown that same level of attention. But then what about Stevie? His concerns seemed genuine when Annabelle surprised him with her disappearance. Then again, if Grey knew about Stevie before, he would have had time to plan to act dismayed about her kidnapping.

Pulling himself out of the bush he was hiding in, James fled to the palace. If The Controller had got wind of his plans, Stevie was in grave danger. He couldn't believe he had been so naïve as to trust anyone else. He had been the one after all to turn Stevie away from the idea of recruiting allies to begin with. Just as he began to pick up his pace, a heavy hand laid itself on his shoulder. Ready to fight, James turned around, all guns blazing. "What's the rush mate? I thought you were going to wait for me," came the familiar voice of an out of breath Grey, who had been very clearly running after James.

"What do you mean what's the rush? Where have you been? We agreed we were meeting at sundown," James replied, relieved that Grey hadn't abandoned him altogether, but still wary about his intentions.

"I know, I got here as fast as I could. Amos scheduled a meeting for tonight days ago, but I had no way to get a message to you. It was all I could do to get here by now."

James hesitated but then nodded. He couldn't see why he'd show up at all if he'd been conspiring with The Controller, and if he was honest with himself, he didn't want to face the mission entirely alone, "You got me really worked up. I was moments away from storming the palace and demanding they tell me where they are keeping Stevie."

Grey took his arm off James' shoulder, "You need to relax. This is only going to work if you keep a cool head. Now let me change into my drudge's blacks before we draw any more attention to ourselves."

Getting into the palace was a lot easier than James had first expected. Just as Grey had predicted, nobody took any notice of two strange drudges wandering the palace corridors. It soon became clear however that finding Stevie was not nearly as simple. While James knew the building was vast from the two times he'd been there, he hadn't quite grasped just how enormous it would be. What felt like hours had gone by and they hadn't so much as seen a rogue drudge cleaning up. By this time of night, everyone would be sleeping, so their best chance of finding Stevie was in the sleeping quarters, but this was also the likely location of the master of the palace. "Do you think they're in the same room?" Grey whispered as they arrived into their fourth living room of the night.

"How am I supposed to know where she is?" James snapped back, furious at the possibility of her sharing a room with that monster.

"Jeez, I was just asking. If she is, we should probably have some sort of backup plan, or should I say, some sort of way of abandoning the plan? We can hardly just bust in there and demand he releases her," he stated, wringing his hands together at the thought of the confrontation.

"Grey, stop asking me so many questions. I know just as much and just as little as you do," James replied, frustrated with his own lack of preparation.

"You are the one who asked me to help you James."

James took a deep breath, realising he was venting his distress at the wrong person, "Sorry Grey. I know you are doing me a solid. Stevie too. It's just been ages and there's no sign of life. I'm beginning to lose..." but before James could finish his apology, a high pitched voice from behind him interrupted them, "Well, well... What are two drudges doing wandering the Palace at this time of the night?"

In unison, James and Grey slowly turned to see a tall thin woman with long black hair, dressed completely in white staring at them.

"Oh, I see, you're not drudges at all, are you... Mr Moore?" James had no idea how this strange Whiteflyer knew his name, but he was sure she wasn't in the slightest bit familiar. "A level four Torpor Whiteflyer impersonating someone so far below them," the woman pointed out, a vicious grin upturning the corners of her mouth. "And you..." she exclaimed, turning on Grey. "I don't imagine you're a drudge either. Are you?" Unsure of what to say, James and Grey just stared at her blankly, their mouths dropped open. "You're lucky The Controller is on the other side of the world. As it is, you'll have another while to come up with a viable excuse to give him as to why you are so far from your world without invitation. From what I can see, you didn't come prepared," she giggled before lifting her hand to summon the air surrounding them, to bound them both together and pull them towards her.

Instinctively, James blocked her air path with his own before she had the chance to even drag them a foot closer. He hadn't seen her photo before during their history lessons, which meant the highest ranking she could have was level 3. He had the advantage of Earth, even though she would have the advantage of experience. Acting fast, he enabled his power source to drag her underground. She wouldn't be able to get out easily, and it would give them the time they needed to escape. "Are you crazy?" Grey yelped, as he blocked the fireballs coming from the sinking woman. "We can't attack another Whiteflyer, Amos will have my head, if The Controller doesn't first."

James threw his eyes up to heaven, "Well if you had a better idea, you weren't very quick to implement it were you? I wasn't just going to let her trap us. We've come too far and she's already caught us. What, did you think she was just going to let us continue home and act like this never happened? It's now or never."

Just as he finished burying the Arcadius Whiteflyer up to her knees, James heard the muffled sounds of reinforcements coming through the palace towards them. "So, now what genius?" Grey turned, still deflecting the fire being shot their way, now from an even angrier source.

"Now...we run!" Without hesitation, both novice Whiteflyers rapidly backed out of the room, keeping their eyes focused on the wailing woman until they turned the corner and she disappeared from sight.

"What's there to smile about?" Grey asked, horrified by the optimistic look on James' face. "We still don't know where Stevie is and there are now numerous Whiteflyers hunting us down. Safe to say, nothing is going in our favour."

James laughed, a slightly hysterical but joyous laugh, before coming to a halt, "Weren't you listening? The Controller is on the other side of the world."

Grey paused alongside him and rested his hands on his knees to try and catch his breath, "Okay, so one thing is going in our favour."

James shook his head, "Nope, not just one. It's like you just said, The Palace's Whiteflyers are hunting us, so we don't need to find Stevie after all. She's coming to us."

Greys face beamed at the realisation that Stevie was in fact a Palace Whiteflyer, "So if she's coming, then why are we running?"

James looked around at the big room they'd stopped in. It was the same dining room he'd first met The Controller in, "We're not running anymore, we are exactly where we need to be. We just needed a head start to set up."

17. "LOOK AT WHAT I'VE DONE TO HER."

As quickly and efficiently as he could, James rearranged the large room, simultaneously taking Grey through his game plan. In some places, he erected walls and doorways and in others, he just moved the furniture or created deep holes in the floor. At night, this was the point of the plan he'd gone over the most in his head. The battle scene. He of course wasn't sure that it would even come to this, but there was always a possibility when so many powerful people were about. He knew he had to come prepared if he wanted any chance of beating them. Of course, The Controller had always been an element in his plans, but it was something he was more than happy to leave out for the real thing. The idea of creating his own battle ground first came to him after waking up from a recurring dream he'd been having about the day he had completed the challenge and become a Whiteflyer. They'd had the luxury of making him squirm and now it was his turn to repay the favour.

James and Grey sat floating in the top corner of the room, waiting for their hunters to find them. James had built a thin wall to cover them with two small eye holes to give them time to suss out the Whiteflyers before they started to attack. "And here I was thinking that it didn't matter whether or not I mastered Earth," Grey remarked, looking out at the completely refreshed dining hall. "Let's be honest, it definitely trumps the rest of the powers. This looks like a completely different room." James smirked. Just recently he had realised the same thing. At first, he was captivated by the possibilities with Water but the more advanced he became, the more he realised that Earth was probably his favourite power. Whether that was because so few people could use it, or because the world was his canvas, he didn't know, but he reckoned it was a bit of both.

"When we are ready, I'm going to call out. We need them all to find us, or we might miss Stevie. I reckon they've spread out to look for us," James explained to an adrenaline filled Grey. "How's your past Whiteflyer knowledge? Would you be able to spot the level 4s? I think I would, but Stevie was always better at that." Grey stayed silent before nodding sharply, "Yeah I would. I would recognise them as being familiar anyway. So, if there are any and if you haven't picked up on them, I'll send them your way. Fire's my specialty, so don't worry about getting charred, I'll have your back." James nodded confidently, "And there's no water in here, so that's one less thing to worry about."

"Ready?" James asked, before screaming the one thing he'd been dying to do since he arrived at the Palace. "Stevie…Stevie…Stevie… We've come to get you out of here. We're in here. Stevie…Stevie," A few moments passed before the first sounds of running came shooting down the hall. James and Grey didn't move a muscle, making sure they weren't seen before they had time to spot their friend. Two Whiteflyers came storming into the room, their radars up, ready for an attack. Then three more joined them, including the black haired woman that had found them before.

"What's this?" a short blonde haired girl in her early 20s asked nobody in particular as she looked around the dining hall. "He's redone the room. They'll be hiding." Stevie hadn't arrived yet but the sounds of footsteps coming towards them hadn't died down, so James grabbed hold of Grey's arm to signal for him to wait. Three more women entered, each one more beautiful than the last.

"Typical Moore," grunted one of them, before James realised who it was. He should have known Tessa wouldn't take his side on this. She'd always been too close to Matthew for James to think she cared about anything other than getting to the top. She turned slowly, monitoring her surroundings, before doing the unthinkable and looking up.

Instantly, she shot a gust of wind towards them shattering their thin cover and knocking them off balance. The other Whiteflyers whipped around in time to witness the blast. Grey lunged forward before he was hit, but James who was still distracted by Tessa's presence got the brunt of it. He was knocked to the ground, where a second Whiteflyer was ready with a burning ball of fire. Luckily, Grey had meant what he'd said about having his back, and the ball went out as quickly as it was thrown, giving James enough time to surround himself in an air bubble. It would burst with just one hit, but it gave him a chance to gather his bearings. This was his course, not theirs, and he wouldn't give them any more advantages.

Picking himself up, James ran behind the first two walls that he had planted. There was an alcove there that was dark enough to make it so he could see out of it, but nobody could see in. He could hear Grey above blocking fireballs and dodging gusts of wind. Cautiously, three of their attackers followed him, and without giving it a second thought, James set them all alight. The day Hatt had set Rebecca on fire he couldn't believe what he was seeing, yet here he was, doing the very same to the three screaming women flailing around in front of him. Realising the big difference, that they knew how to defend themselves and extinguish the flames and Rebecca didn't, he crawled out of his hold and moved onto the next area of his makeshift arena before any of them had calmed down long enough to do the same thing.

Watching where he stood, James jumped along the sturdy sections of the floor, making sure to dodge the hidden potholes. This part of his arena was the most challenging to create and he didn't want to give away its secrets before his enemies succumbed to it. Just as he made it to the other side, two women, one who he had burnt and one who he had never seen before came bursting around the corner. The curvier of the two, who sported freshly made red blisters, heaved the air around her with a vengeance. Building up speed and momentum, she let out her anger in James' direction. A whirlpool stronger and faster than he had witnessed before dragged him backwards. With no quick way to stop it and not enough notice, James ran forwards, holding onto every last ounce of strength he had. If the whirlpool pulled him in, he'd set off his own traps, and capture himself. Luckily, the woman stepped forward with excitement at seeing James squirm and the light layer of stone beneath her feet crumbled, and she disappeared from sight.

In shock, the second woman faltered, unsure of what had happened to her friend. She stared at the ground confused before realising what James had done. With a moment's thought, she too manipulated the air around her but instead of releasing it at James, she let out her frustration at the floor. All of the light layers of stone broke with the force, and she was free to continue in James' direction in no danger of falling. "Damn it!" James muttered under his breath as he continued through the maze. "That should have caught more than one."

"A little bit of help up here," Grey shouted, just as James broke free of the makeshift low ceilings that he had covered the first half of the room with, allowing him to fly back up to help his friend. Back to back, they threw fire ball after fire ball at their enemies, incapacitating all of the original Whiteflyers that were still standing. Unfortunately, just as the last one hit the floor, five new women replaced them.

"How many Whiteflyers does he have here?" James yelled amongst the bangs.

"I don't know, but I can hear more coming," Grey, who was closest to the door replied.

"Get to the hatch," James screamed, realising the odds were increasingly growing against them. Happily obeying, Grey shot off to the farthest side of the room, unsure of what was coming, but expecting the worst. James had made it clear, while he was setting the room up, that if he signalled for Grey to get to the hatch, it meant business.

James put up a shield of air and waited. Waited until the Whiteflyers nearly at the room had entered, waited until the opportune time to strike. Not paying attention to who had come in, completely focusing his energy on incapacitating their pursuers, he focused his power source on the ceiling. He thought of Liza still lost, and the ceiling rumbled. He thought of Anne separated from the love of her life and the look in her face when he told her she may have to relocate, and once more the ceiling rumbled. Finally, he thought of The Controller taking Stevie, and as his heart raced and his anger elevated, the ceiling exploded into pieces.

Everyone around James dropped to the floor as chunks of rock came lashing down, catching limbs and covering bodies in leftover debris. The screams were short lived as each Whiteflyer fell unconscious. Bursting the thick bubble of air around him, James ran to pull Grey from the two-foot-thick hatch he'd created to protect him. "It's over, but who knows for how long. We've got to get out of here before they wake up or before more of them join us," James gasped, out of breath and low on energy. "They have all been coming from the same direction. I reckon we head that way and give it one last push to find her, and if we still can't, we may have no choice but to leave." Grey didn't answer, instead glaring dumbfoundedly at the far side of the room. His face was white, and his hand gently shook. James turned to see what he was staring at, unsure of what could cause such a reaction.

"What did you do?" Grey whispered, just as James' eyes caught sight of the reason behind his emotions. Stevie was lying by the door, covered in blood. Her leg turned upwards in an unnatural state. A terrible wave of disgust rose up James' body, and spewed out his mouth. He scrunched his eyes and tip toed forward, terrified to get closer to her, but unable to stay put. Grey beat him to it and lifted her frail body from the rocks. "We can't stay here," he stated matter of factly, holding Stevie tightly as he led the way from the demolition site. James followed blindly, unaware of where he was going and uncaring to what would happen if anyone else was to find them.

They'd walked a while before Grey stopped outside in a small garden and lay Stevie down. "Snap out of it!" he demanded, whipping his head around to face James. "Stevie is already immobile, don't make things even more difficult by zoning out with her."

James rubbed his face with his hands, "I didn't look. I should have looked. Why didn't I check who came into the room? Look at what I've done to her." Staring down at Stevie as he ordered Grey to do the very same thing, James snapped back to reality. "But that can't be," he mumbled, as he kneeled down beside her, brushing the hair from her face as if it would make all the difference to her debilitated appearance. "She's already healing."

Grey shook his head, "Yes James, that tends to happen when you can't die. It won't stop the pain though." James remembered seeing Rebecca after she had been burnt to what would have been definite death. She had no visible scars or reminders of what had happened, but at the time he had never imagined it took this short a time to heal. Relieved, he took a deep breath and concentrated on helping Stevie's healing process. Closing one eye, he cracked her leg's bone back into place and then moved onto her out of place hand. He was still shaken over what he had put her through, but the realisation that she'd be back to normal soon enough gave him the strength to focus on the task at hand.

James took off the white t-shirt beneath his robe and ran to dampen it in the fountain nearby, momentarily forgetting he could have summoned it in a heartbeat. Carefully wiping the blood from Stevie's forehead, he gently whispered, "You are safe now," reassuring himself more than anyone else. Patting her reddening cheeks clean, his heart stopped as her eyes opened. A gush of emotions poured into James' whole self. It was unlike anything he'd ever felt before and without even registering what he was doing he had leaned in to kiss her. Her lips felt softer than he had ever dared imagined. They moved in rhythm with his as if they'd kissed one hundred times before. For a brief moment everything was right again. James had finally found his way home.

Realising what was happening, James built up all the strength he had and pulled away. This wasn't fair. It felt more perfect than anything, but at the same time, he still hadn't made things right with Liza. It wasn't fair on either of them. "She's safe," Stevie croaked quietly, reading James' mind once more. "Liza never died. She's still on earth."

Unsure of what he was hearing, James leant in, "But how..."

Stevie smiled, "He keeps a register. The Controller. Everyone who's ever died and where they ended up is filed away. I checked it twice, she survived the crash."

A weight, bigger than James had realised existed, detached itself from his back and floated free. There was a reason he got butterflies when Stevie smiled and why he couldn't stand being without her. There was a reason he was so quick to rescue her, without still having managed to look for Liza. It was her, from the moment he saw her in the hospital. It had always been her.

"Erm, excuse me," Grey interrupted. "As much as I want to stand here and be a third wheel. We've got a swarm of venomous Whiteflyers after us and considering Stevie is healing, I'd guess that some of them are too." Stevie got up to stand but fell back, still weak from her more serious injuries and from the healing process.

"Don't you dare," James ordered. "The least I can do is carry you out of here."

Grey led the way out of the palace grounds, under the experienced guidance of Stevie. "How do you know your way around so well? You've only lived here for a week or two," Grey asked, after being directed through a second hidden door.

"After the first day of tantrums, I decided to change tactics and use my time wisely. I've spent every moment alone here, exploring this place. You wouldn't believe some of the stuff I've found out," Stevie explained, her voice evidently less exhausted than when she had first woken up. "I discovered that there are a lot of secrets that even Whiteflyers are not privy to."

James was about to question her further on everything she knew, but instead decided to keep it light. There would be time enough to find out everything. For now, it was enough that she was safe, "So did you find out about your mum then?"

Stevie smiled, turning up one side of her face and nodded, "Yes I did and she's in Tartarus like I thought, but god knows when I'll get the chance to find her now. They'll take away our Whiteflyer status for sure once they find us."

Unexpectedly, Grey made a stop and turned to look them both in the eye, "They won't take away anything, because we aren't going to let them find us. We haven't even started this, we've got work to do."

James couldn't help but admire Grey's resilience, but he wasn't totally confident that they could stay hidden, "Well then, where do we go? We can't stay in Arcadius, that's for sure. We could go back to Torpor, we'd have a better chance..."

Grey interrupted, "No, I've been to Torpor. It's too civilised, we'll stand out. We'll have to go to Tartarus."

Stevie's face beamed at the thought and as James couldn't think of any other alternative he agreed, "Tartarus it is, but we've got to act fast. We need to get to the clock before The Controller's Whiteflyers wake up and figure out where we are heading.

Stevie smiled and carefully freed herself from James' arms, "Yes, so maybe I should take it from here."

Quickly and quietly, Stevie took Grey and James out onto the street and headed for Big Ben. It didn't seem like anyone was in front of or behind them, but they'd no idea how long that would last, so they had to move fast. "I'll go through first," Grey declared, when the gateway to Tartarus came into sight. "Suss out the situation on the other side. Stevie, count to one hundred and follow behind. That will give me some time to clear the way if I need to. And then James, you do the same. James didn't mind going last. If anyone was to get caught before they made it out, he'd rather it be him. Before they'd even reached their destination, Grey rose up in the air and carried on forward, "Remember, count before coming through."

Once the door closed behind him, James nervously began the count in his head, but was soon interrupted by a fireball flying right by him. He turned to see half a dozen of the women he'd just collapsed the roof on top of coming towards him. Anger raging in their eyes. "Go Stevie go," he demanded, pushing her forward.

"But Grey said one hundred seconds. What if he hasn't..." But before she could finish, James cut her off, "I said go Stevie."

Reluctantly, Stevie did as she was asked, and James was left alone to slow down the oncoming adversaries. He shot streams of fire in their direction and sent a gust of wind to blow them off their feet. But it was six against one, he couldn't stop them all from making their way to the clock in time. Stevie and Grey were on the other side waiting, he couldn't risk the Whiteflyers coming through after him. He needed to destroy the pathway. Thinking quickly, James attempted something he was completely unsure would work, timing was everything. He moved the hands of the clock to 6 and climbed into the portal to the other worlds, careful not to close the door behind him, and closed his eyes. He pictured what he needed to happen as he willed it to, and his power source followed.

Using the power of Earth, James sheared the top half of Big Ben's clock tower from its base and with Air he forced it to fly upwards, away from the anchor that it had been bound to for so long. When he was high enough, he withdrew his power source and readied himself for the inevitable drop. Gravity took over. Big Ben, no longer under his influence, crashed towards the ground. Opening his eyes, he shut the door. The short lived feeling in his stomach, that he was falling, disappeared. He was on steady ground. He was in Tartarus.

ABOUT THE AUTHOR

Kieva McLaughlin was born in Dublin, Ireland. She studied Journalism in University and later went on to get her MSc in Marketing. Since an early age, Kieva was drawn to books that didn't reflect normal, everyday life. Fantasy books, stories set in a different era and war novels have always been amongst her favourites.

After waking from a vivid night of dreaming, Kieva jotted down what memories she had left of a sleep filled with afterlives, flying soldiers, fire throwers and love. Two years later, the first book of three, Torpor, was born.

Printed in Great Britain
by Amazon